HOW YA LIKE ME NOW

BRENDAN HALPIN

Farrar Straus Giroux / *New York*

4
dkol

Copyright © 2007 by Brendan Halpin
All rights reserved
Distributed in Canada by Douglas & McIntyre Ltd.
Printed in the United States of America
Designed by Jay Colvin
First edition, 2007
1 3 5 7 9 10 8 6 4 2

www.fsgkidsbooks.com

Library of Congress Cataloging-in-Publication Data
Halpin, Brendan, date.
    How ya like me now / Brendan Halpin.— 1st ed.
        p.   cm.
    Summary: After his father dies and his mother goes into rehab, Eddie
moves from the suburbs into his cousin's Boston loft, where he gradually
adjusts to being one of the few white kids in a progressive school, and
learns how to feel like a normal teenager.
    ISBN-13: 978-0-374-33495-6
    ISBN-10: 0-374-33495-1
    [1. Emotional problems—Fiction.   2. Schools—Fiction.   3. City
and town life—Massachusetts—Fiction.   4. Cousins—Fiction.
5. Race relations—Fiction.   6. Interpersonal relations—Fiction.
7. Mothers and sons—Fiction.   8. Boston (Mass.)—Fiction.]   I. Title:
How you like me now.   II. Title.

PZ7.H16674 Ho 2007
[Fic]—dc22

                                                          2006040989

For Peg Halpin, who did it right

Special thanks to Kyle Olson

HOW YA LIKE ME NOW

1

EDDIE SHIFTED FROM ONE FOOT TO
the other on his front porch, trying to keep warm, while his
aunt Lily clutched her coffee cup. "Thanks for coming to get
me," he said to her.

Aunt Lily's face got all twisted like she was about to cry.
This made Eddie feel awkward. She looked like she was fighting to keep the tears in. Eddie hoped she won. "I'm just sorry
it took . . . it took something like this . . ."

"Don't feel bad," Eddie said. Because, he thought, it's all my
fault anyway. He tried to push that thought way down deep
inside him, but it kept creeping back up. "I'll just get my
stuff," he said.

"Do you want me to help you with that, Eddie?"

No, Eddie thought, nobody comes in the house. That had
been the rule pretty much since Dad died, and even though
Mom was locked up somewhere and the house was going to

have lots of people coming through it pretty soon, it seemed kind of weird to break the rule in his last moments in the house. "I . . . Thanks, Aunt Lily. I, uh, I guess I want to do it by myself."

"I understand. I'll wait here," Aunt Lily said. She sat down on the step, took the lid off her coffee, and blew some steam away.

Inside, Eddie was confronted by a mess of stuff on the floor—magazines, soda cans, beer cans, wine bottles, liquor bottles, pizza boxes. Tomorrow was supposed to be his big cleanup day. Oh well. He walked past the kitchen and saw the dishes he hadn't done and never would.

He walked into his room. His clean laundry was folded on his bed. He was glad he'd done it yesterday, because now he had clean clothes. It would have been even more embarrassing to show up with a bag full of dirty clothes. He wondered if he had enough clothes for how long he'd be living in Boston without Mom. Six weeks? Six months? Forever? How long till Mom got clean, till she wanted him again, till she wanted him more than the drugs, till she had enough money to get someplace to live?

He remembered the last time it felt like Mom cared more about him than getting high. It was a long time ago. After Dad died, but still a long time ago. Ever since Dad died of cancer, leaving them his life insurance policy and a nearly full bottle of OxyContin they gave him for his pain, Mom had been getting high, and after a while it fell to Eddie to keep the house together. He had to do his own laundry, steal Mom's ATM card so that he could buy food from the Stop & Shop, and then cook and clean. Eventually, it was like he was basically alone here. Or, anyway, that was what he told himself. It got to the point where he worked out this whole fantasy about how he was an orphan but nobody knew it, and he was living on his own and taking care of himself at age fifteen, and he started hating to even see Mom, because it was a lot easier to imagine she was dead than it was to deal with her alive. Fortunately, she was almost always asleep when Eddie left for school, and she was out for the evening by the time Eddie got home from band practice, newspaper, yearbook, or any of the other activities he signed up for to keep him away from the house five days a week. So the fantasy was working great, but at some point Mom totally stopped even trying to pay bills, and Eddie was so busy with everything else that he didn't know it. All he did with the mail that piled up was to put it on Dad's desk. He guessed he probably should have stolen the checkbook and paid the bills. And then maybe everything would still be fine instead of Mom being in rehab, Eddie heading for Boston, and God knows who moving into this house.

Eddie looked around his room at his trophies from camp in sixth grade, at his PlayStation 2, his TV, his poster of Tom Brady. He remembered how much fun he'd had winning the relay race at camp, how happy he was that summer. He remembered the day Dad brought the PS2 home and they'd played Madden till midnight. He remembered when the Pats won their first Super Bowl, and how he and Dad went all the way in to Boston on the commuter rail just to see the Pats go by and wave, and to see the trophy, and how it was freezing cold but everything in the world felt perfect that day. He reached for his soccer championship trophy to begin packing it and everything else, but once the trophy was in his hand, he found he didn't want to pack it. Instead, he carefully and methodically broke it. Then he took the PS2, placed it on the floor, and destroyed it with a quick stomp. He liked the crunchy sound of the plastic breaking. He carefully took down the Tom Brady poster and tore it neatly and precisely in half, and then tore the pieces in half, and repeated this again and again until Tom Brady was practically confetti. He attacked the rest of his possessions with the same calm and precision, and twenty minutes later, a duffel bag full of clothes sat on his bed next to his desk, and every other single thing in the room was broken.

Eddie surveyed what used to be his room and felt like he'd just woken up. He looked around at the wreckage, at everything he had destroyed. Good, he thought. Now it matches the rest of my life.

He pulled a snotty tissue out of his pocket and blew his nose, and wiped his eyes on the sleeves of his Red Sox shirt.

He put his coat on, grabbed the duffel bag, and joined his aunt on the porch.

Aunt Lily smiled at him. "Ready?" she asked.

Eddie didn't know if he was ready or not, but he nodded anyway. He tried to think good things. It was a new year—well, a new calendar year, even if it was halfway through the school year—and he was going to a new school, and maybe everything would be different and better. He held on to that thought for about ten seconds before he started feeling sad again.

It seemed like a long drive to Boston. They rode in silence for a while, and then Eddie looked over and saw Aunt Lily's face twisting up again. Oh boy, he thought, here it comes. "Eddie," Aunt Lily said, "I'm just really sorry that it got to this point, that we weren't around to help out sooner. I just . . . I mean, Jesus, I knew it was bad, but I swear to God, Eddie, if I'd had any idea, I would have . . . I . . . We let you down, Eddie. I'm sorry about that."

Eddie remembered Mom screaming, "Mind your own god-damn business!" into the phone the last time Aunt Lily had called. He didn't blame his aunt—what was she supposed to do, anyway? And besides, it was Eddie's problem. "Don't worry about it. It's not your fault."

Aunt Lily gave him a watery gaze. "You're sweet, Eddie, you really are. And I just want you to know that we're going to do everything we can for you. I mean, Brian's already been on the phone lining up somebody you can talk to about this, you know, so you don't have to carry it all by yourself."

Oh great, Eddie thought. Just what I need. His stomach tightened. Don't you get it? he wanted to yell. Not talking about it was the only thing that made me able to deal with it. Talking about it would be a big waste. All he wanted was to be a normal kid, or as normal a kid as he could possibly be, any-way, and normal kids didn't talk about stuff. Normal kids just got up and went to school and did what they had to do, and they didn't have to worry about the laundry or grocery shop-ping. That's all he wanted. What good was talking about it going to do?

2

IT WAS CASUAL FRIDAY. ALEX GOT off the Silver Line bus, adjusted his backpack, reached inside his coat to straighten the tie he'd forgotten he wasn't wearing, checked his ID badge, and walked into the Parley Funds Tower.

Alex entered the CUE ONLY elevator. He waited for the doors to begin shutting, then slapped the inside of the closing doors and watched them pop back open. As the doors closed again, he could hear the grumpy old security guard yelling, "Don't play with the elevator! I will get your principal down here . . ." and Alex smiled to himself.

Alone in the elevator, he pressed 2, and in three seconds the doors opened again. Alex approached the double glass doors that were the entryway of his school. They said CENTER FOR URBAN EDUCATION in white stick-on letters. If you looked closely, you could still see the outline of PARLEY FUNDS, which they had scraped off the door three years ago.

Alex swiped his ID badge through the card reader, heard the click as the door unlocked, and yanked the door open. He headed down the carpeted hallway toward Human Resources, which was what normal, non-corny schools called the Office. He and his parents had a meeting with Mr. Paulson, the chief executive officer (or principal) before school this morning, but Alex had talked Dad into letting him stop for coffee. Because he wanted some coffee to start the day, because the barista at the Melville's next door to school was incredibly hot, and especially because he didn't want anybody in his advisory—or anybody else, for that matter—to see him walk into school with Mom and Dad.

In Human Resources, Mr. Paulson, the principal (even after a year and a half here, Alex couldn't bring himself to call him the CEO), was sitting behind his desk and saying something to Alex's dad. Paulson was a tall guy in his forties with salt-and-pepper hair who wore a gray or dark blue suit with a red or yellow tie even on casual Friday. Today it was dark blue suit, red tie. "Alex! It's a beautiful day for learning here in the Hub of the Universe, and welcome to the best school in the world," Paulson said. "Your father and I were just discussing whether your grades this quarter are going to improve."

Paulson was so corny.

Alex knew this meeting wasn't really about him, so he didn't take the bait and just said, "Good morning, Mr. Paulson! It's a fine day in the Athens of America." Mom rolled her eyes, and Dad was fighting really hard not to smile.

"Certainly is, my young friend, it certainly is," Mr. Paulson replied.

Alex sat down, and Mr. Paulson said, "Alex, before we began addressing the subject of your grades, we were going over preparations for your cousin Edward's arrival here at the Center for Urban Education.

"Now, as I have told you and your parents, the founders held to the belief that no student could possibly transfer into this school, especially sophomore year, and be successful, because our standards and expectations are, as you know, quite a bit more stringent than the average school's. But given the special circumstances, I believe this is a case that merits an exception to the policy. However, to ensure that Edward will achieve his full potential, we are, with your parents' permission, going to place him with you in advisory 212 so that you can guide him through the orientation process."

Great, Alex thought. Advisory was the funnest part of the day, and now they had to ruin it. Paulson went on about communicating clear expectations for academics and behavior, Mom and Dad went on about easing the transition and about how Eddie'd been through such a tough time, and all Alex could think was that advisory was going to start to suck. He figured he'd better enjoy it today.

Finally the adults shut up and told him he was free to go. He found the heavy wooden door of Room 212 shut, and this immediately cheered Alex up. Whenever the advisory door was shut, it was a sign that something interesting was going on, even now, fifteen minutes before anybody even had to be at school.

Sure enough, when Alex opened the door he saw Kelvin seated in a chair with his hair half braided and half sticking straight up. He looked sort of like he'd gotten an electric shock just on the left side of his head.

Gisela was standing over him, laughing, while Kelvin was pleading, "Come on, Gisela, man, you gotta finish it! I'll get sent home, and my dad ain't having that!"

Gisela said, "Guess you shoulda thought of that before you started talkin' trash about Cape Verdeans!"

"I wasn't talking trash!" Kelvin had a mischievous grin on his face. "I'm just sayin', you can't talk about 'as a young black woman' when you're some kind of half-Spanish Puerto Rican wannabe."

Gisela looked around the room. "And this fool expects me to finish braiding his hair. Talking 'bout I'm half-Spanish. Cape Verde is in *Africa*, Kelvin. *Africa*. Don't hate just because your crispy black ass never been out of Mattapan."

"Fine, fine." Kelvin looked around. "Aisha! Strong black woman. You can finish braiding my hair."

Aisha didn't even have to say "Boy, you must be crazy," because the look on her face said it all.

Savon looked up from his book and called out, "It's eight-fifteen. You better get somebody to clean up them naps before eight-thirty. You know Paulson's gonna stick his head in here all 'My young friend, this simply does not constitute a professional appearance. Let's call your father.'"

"Shut up, Savon, man! Tanya, Tanya, you want to braid my hair, right?"

"I braid hair for a *job*, Kelvin. You want to pay me what I earn in the shop?"

Everybody, even Kenisha and Hanh, who were always studying, was watching and laughing, and Alex quickly forgot about Eddie. Even Savon, who studied less than Kenisha and Hanh but still more than anybody else, and enough that he was always Alex's first choice when he needed to copy homework or cheat on a quiz, had actually closed his book so he could concentrate on dissing Kelvin properly.

"Shoot, you think Kelvin's got any money? You must be crazy! You seen his house? It's that thing out back, with the big plastic lid to keep the rats out? Big ol' blue truck comes to empty it out every Wednesday!"

The whole advisory laughed.

"Yeah, that's right, Savon, I got no money. That's why your mom hired my dad to sue King Kong for child support!" Kelvin responded.

This led to a round of "Ohhhhhhs!" from everybody, and Alex, plopping into the chair next to Savon, said, "I think Kelvin just called you a monkey!"

Savon just smiled, waved his hand, opened his math book up, and said, "This monkey got a four-point-oh GPA, so I guess Kelvin's dumber than a monkey."

"Aggh! Come on, Gisela, man, please, I'm sorry, just finish it!" Kelvin begged.

"Not until you say, 'Cape Verde is in Africa, which is something my ignorant ghetto ass should know.'"

"Ahhh! Fine! Capeverdeisinafricawhichissomethingmyignorantghettoassshouldknow. Okay? Please, Gisela!"

"All right, then," Gisela said, and started working on the unbraided side of Kelvin's head.

Gisela braided, making sure to pull Kelvin's hair really tight so he was wincing in pain the whole time, while Alex and Aisha made fun of Kelvin, and Savon looked up from his book every couple of minutes to dis him again.

Just after Gisela finished, their advisor, Mr. Harrison, walked in. Harrison was a short, red-haired white guy with more freckles than anyone Alex had ever seen. "Good morning, everybody! It's eight-thirty, official start of the work day here at the Center for Urban Education, and I'm happy to see so many of you here. Remember, pizza at the end of the quarter if we have the fewest tardies in the school. Right now we're tied with the 256 advisory."

None of them said anything or looked up from their books. "Yes, I'm fine," Mr. Harrison said. "Thanks very much! What a pleasure it is to work with such a polite group of young people!"

"Come on, Harry," Alex said. "You want us to all say, 'Good morning, Mr. Harrison,' like we're in kindergarten or something?"

"I'd settle for any kind of greeting," Harrison said, "and don't call me Harry. I hate that."

This got Kelvin, who was probably close to a foot taller than Harrison, to pipe up with "What up, shortstop?"

The part of Harrison's face that was not covered in freckles turned bright red. "Well, it's something, anyway, but I don't think I'm going to thank you, Kelvin."

"You're welcome."

"Annnnyway, listen up, folks, important announcements

from the CEO." Harrison looked over the piece of paper in his hand, "Okay, blah blah blah, no . . . okay, told you that yesterday . . . okay, T passes are available in Human Resources, please stop by today and pick them up. That's all I got. What about you? Anybody have anything important they'd like to mention?"

Alex figured he'd better get this over with. He knew this was pointless, but he should probably say it anyway. "Yeah," Alex said, "uh, I just wanted to remind everybody that my cousin is starting here on Monday. Please give him a break and don't clown him too much."

"Oh, snap," Kelvin said, "another little Alex! He's gonna have a hard time!"

"Nah, nah, guys, really," Alex said. "He's had a hard time already."

"Yeah, but, you know," Kelvin said, "if he's gonna hang in 212, he's gonna have to be able to take it and dish it out. See, that's Gisela's problem. Dishes it out, can't take it."

"Oooh, I knew I should've left your head half-nappy," Gisela said. "Don't ask me to help you again."

"Well, listen," Mr. Harrison said, "you guys are way over the line in here all the time, and I let it go because I know it's your twisted way of expressing affection. But somebody who's new to the mix in here might not get that, so try not to level this kid in his first week here."

"Yo, Alex, is your cousin cute?" Hanh asked.

"Aww, I don't know. I mean, he's not ugly or anything. But I don't really know if he's cute or not."

"Well, if there's a family resemblance he probably ain't cute, but I hope he is," Gisela said. "Because I am getting tired of seeing all of y'all's ugly faces every morning."

"Oooh! I heard that," Hanh offered.

"Yeah?" Kelvin asked. "How you think us boys feel walking into the dog pound every morning, talking about, 'Ooh, that one ain't got her shots!' " He pointed at Aisha as he said this, and she began to rise out of her seat to hit Kelvin, but Mr. Harrison put a hand on her shoulder.

"Okay, okay, let's not give Kelvin the smacking he so richly deserves this morning. It doesn't contribute to a positive working environment. And speaking of which, it's transition time."

Everybody groaned. "Come on, Mr. Harrison, man, this is so corny!" Kelvin said.

"I'm sorry, Kelvin, but I'm having difficulty hearing you when you're not using professional language. Would you like to rephrase your comment?"

Kelvin rolled his eyes, took a deep breath, and said, "Mr. Harrison. By now we all know how to use professional language in class."

"Yeah," Alex said, "why can't we just talk normal in here and then talk CUE-style for the rest of the day?"

Harrison looked at him blankly. "I mean," Alex continued, "I think we make better use of our time in here when it's an informal environment."

"It does get tiring," Aisha popped up.

"Must we go over this again? One of the primary purposes

of advisory is to help us all transition from home mode to school mode. All I'm asking is that you ease into formality in the last five minutes."

"Corny," Kelvin said, then added before Harrison could object, "I mean, it seems unnecessary."

"Well, Kelvin, that is where you and I part company," Harrison said.

Gisela raised her hand.

"Yes, Gisela?"

"I seen—sorry, saw this HBO documentary about stockbrokers, and they be—they swear all the time on the job. So it doesn't seem like they actually use the professional language that the school thinks we should be using."

Everybody looked at Mr. Harrison. He took a deep breath and said, "Listen, Gisela, how many of the stockbrokers on that show looked like the students in this room?"

"You mean Alex, or everybody else?" Harrison didn't answer. "I don't know—a handful." Alex thought it was interesting that Gisela somehow didn't count Tanya as white, even though she was way paler than he was.

"Okay. Once you get your stockbroker job, you can drop f-bombs every other word for all I care. What we're trying to do is to make sure you can get through the interview, that you know how to present yourself in a way that's going to impress people. Now, maybe it's not fair that you guys have to do more than other kids to impress people in those positions, but that's the world we live in, the world we're trying to get you guys to run someday, so you can do a better job than the people running it now."

Nobody was really convinced by this, but it did kind of take the fun out of arguing. "All right," Harrison said, "it's now time for you guys to actually do some work, so get out of here so I can teach some first-year associates."

The students from 212 gathered up their books and slumped out of the door to class as the tiny ninth-graders filed in, and Mr. Harrison said, "Yes! The Odyssey of Homer! Let's put out a Cyclops's eye this morning, shall we?"

3

AUNT LILY HAD FINALLY FINISHED
with her third version of the big speech about how Eddie
should consider himself part of this family now, and he would
be welcome in this house for as long as he needed to stay. Now
Eddie was following his cousin Alex, who he hadn't seen since
Dad's funeral except at that one Fourth of July when Mom got
drunk and yelled and they had to leave, on a big tour of the
house. Well, it wasn't really a house. Of course, they couldn't
live in a house like normal people. It was just a big open space
inside an old factory that you got to by taking this gigantic
elevator that you had to haul on a big strap to open. Weird.

When Dad was alive, Mom always talked about her artsy-
fartsy sister, and how she couldn't understand why she'd want
to live in the city with all the crime and bad schools and drugs.
It was kind of funny now that Eddie thought about it, only
not exactly ha-ha funny, since Mom was the one who actually

got arrested for passing a fake OxyContin prescription. So much for the safe suburbs.

Alex was saying something about how his dad framed up all the walls so everybody could have some privacy, and Eddie looked at the wall in the bedroom he and Alex would share. It was really thin. He wondered if he'd hear Aunt Lily and Uncle Brian having sex. That idea made him very, very uncomfortable.

But so did being here. He felt really strange, like everything he thought he knew about his life was wrong. It was like he had been killed just as he'd reached the end of a level in a video game, and somebody had pressed the continue button, and he'd ended up in a different game altogether. Was this really his life now? Who was this kid with the duffel bag in his hand listening to his cousin talk about God knows what? And how messed up was it that fending for himself while his mom did drugs felt like the normal life, and this one was the weird one?

Alex was smiling and trying to make some kind of joke, but Eddie could barely hear him. He was angry. The only place where anything ever made sense was school, and now he couldn't even go to his own school because he had to live here. He was glad he'd had somebody to call when the cops asked if he had any family in the area, anybody he could stay with, or should they call DSS for a foster home, but he hated having to live here, he hated Mom for causing this whole situation, and he hated Alex and everybody else who felt sorry for him. He wanted to scream at Alex, at Aunt Lily, at Uncle Brian, that no one needed to feel sorry for him, that he had been just fine by himself, that he wasn't some baby that needed people to look out for him. Well, except for that part about paying the bills.

But, of course, Eddie was not a screamer, he never had been. Even when things got really terrible he would say something to Mom in this meek little-kid voice, and then she would yell and he would cry. He sometimes saw those people on *Jerry Springer* or whatever shouting at their brothers and sisters or their boyfriends or girlfriends, or their brothers and sisters who were also their boyfriends and girlfriends, and he wondered how it would feel to yell at somebody like that. He figured he'd never know. So he didn't scream. He said nothing.

4

ALEX WAS TRYING HARD TO BE NICE,
even though he was getting kind of annoyed. He was showing
Eddie around, but Eddie wasn't really saying anything, and
Alex was pretty sure Eddie was turning his nose up at everything, like we don't live like this in the suburbs, why don't you
eat normal food, why don't you have a normal room like in my
stupid house in the suburbs . . . well, whatever.

It was just that Alex was giving up his room, or at least sharing it, and he had gone to all these meetings with Mom and
Dad and Paulson to try to get Eddie admitted to CUE as
some kind of fake sibling, and it's not like they were rich anyway, and now Mom and Dad were going to be spending more
money to feed Eddie, which meant less stuff for Alex, and
Eddie was just being a jerk. Alex made a joke that Eddie didn't
seem to hear, and Alex stopped talking for a second and tried
to imagine if he had to go live at Eddie's house because his

dad was dead and his mom was in rehab. He'd probably be pretty angry. Actually, he'd be a total dick. This thought made him feel a little better about Eddie.

Still, the kid was strange. When the grand tour was over, Eddie lay down on his brand-new futon (Alex thought he should get the new futon and Eddie should get his old one, but Mom and Dad had just given him the "We're so disappointed in you" look when he'd said that) and stared at the ceiling without saying anything.

After a few minutes of silence, Alex felt uncomfortable. "So," he said, "any questions?"

Eddie was quiet, and Alex was wondering whether he should repeat what he'd said or maybe leave the room for a while when Eddie came back with "What did you say the name of your school is again? Center for something?"

Alex loved this more than anything. "FA-CUE."

Eddie clenched his jaw, and his ears turned bright red, and he said, "You don't have to be like that. It's just a question."

Alex laughed. "No! No! That's the name of my school! Francis Abernathy Center for Urban Education! FA-CUE!"

Eddie sat up, looking like he'd just heard something Alex said for the first time. "You're kidding, right?"

"No! Really! Our founders were so grateful to Mayor Abernathy for taking the skyscraper and giving them the space that they named the school after him! Nobody thought of it until kids started going there! It was mad funny! Every time anybody asked where you went to school, you could be all 'FA-CUE!' His name's not on the door anymore, but it's still on all the official school stationery because they ordered so much of it at the beginning."

"FA-CUE," Eddie said. "I like it. It beats OHS, which is what we call . . . called my . . . my old school. Listen, can I ask you something?"

"Of course! I am the urban answer man!"

"Not to be racial or anything, but, um, how many white kids go to this school?"

"I don't know. Maybe twenty or thirty? There's just me and one other girl in my advisory."

"But it's like . . . it's a good school and everything?"

"Yeah, well, most of the kids who can get into the exam schools go there instead. I personally had the test scores but not the GPA to get a spot at an exam school, which Mom had plenty to say about, believe me. But, yeah, FA-CUE is a really good school, I mean, they expect us to all go to college and stuff."

Eddie was silent. Alex wondered what he was thinking. Mom said everybody in Oldham was white, so Eddie probably thought 50 Cent was going to try to shoot him as he walked down the hall or some corny thing like that. Alex wanted to explain, but whenever he tried to think of a way to tell Eddie that he could expect to be teased about his race every day, but so could Kelvin and Hanh and Gisela, and that it didn't really matter because . . . yeah, there was really no way to explain it. Eddie was just going to have to experience it for himself. Alex hoped Eddie did better than that clenching-his-jaw, ears-turning-red thing he constantly did, because if he didn't, he was going to have a really long semester.

5

ALEX LOANED EDDIE A TIE, AND
Eddie put on khakis and a blue oxford shirt and his dad's
loafers that were still about a size too big for him. He hoped
he was wearing acceptable business attire as he got ready for
his first day at school. He wondered what it would be like going to school in the abandoned offices of some bankrupt mu-
tual fund company (or two floors' worth of abandoned offices,
anyway—Alex told him the rest of the tower was occupied by
real companies). Alex wasn't much help because he'd never
been to a regular public high school like OHS.

OHS had those long, long, long hallways, three floors of
them, and the rows of lockers, and the cafeteria, and the gym,
and the clear borders between the jocks and the stoners and
the band geeks and the plain old grinds, which is what Eddie
had been, which was kind of strange since he was also in band,
but, pathetically, he didn't even fit in with the band geeks.

Still, Eddie had known exactly where he fit in at OHS, and it was strangely comfortable to have a place and know that you belonged in it, even if it wasn't really a nice place. Now he'd have to start this whole business over again, and whenever he asked Alex about normal high school stuff like where the stoners hung out, Alex just looked at him blankly like he didn't understand. "It's really not that kind of place," Alex would say. "I can't explain, you'll just have to see."

So on Monday morning, Alex and Eddie had their bowls of organic cinnamon cereal, which Eddie had been afraid of, but which turned out to be good. For the first time since he could remember, Eddie did not eat his before-school breakfast sitting on his bed watching *SportsCenter*. Instead, he and Alex sat at the kitchen table in the corner of the loft with the big windows behind them and Aunt Lily and Uncle Brian passing sections of the paper around. Eddie grabbed the sports pages and found that things were a lot less interesting without the ESPN anchor guys making jokes.

"Okay, boys, it's seven forty-five, you'd better go. Eddie, if Alex tells you he always stops at Melville's for coffee in the morning, ignore him. I certainly don't want you to be late on your first day."

"Mom, in the business world, people stop and get coffee before work, *and* they have flex time. I'm just saying, if the Francis Abernathy Center for Urban Education wants to be all like 'we're like the business world, we're preparing you to compete in the new millennium,' then they ought to ease up about the time. Nobody punches a clock in an office. And anyway, I was only late once."

"Well, I'm not going to argue, Alex. I'm sure Mr. Paulson would love to discuss this with you some Saturday morning if you're late again. Just don't drag Eddie into this particular fight for an important principle. Now get out of here!" She smiled as she said the last part.

Aunt Lily hugged Alex, who hugged her back, and then came over and hugged Eddie, who kind of wanted a hug, but from his mom, so he just stood there stiff and didn't return the hug.

"Have a good day!" she said. "I love you boys!"

"Love you too, Mom," Alex called as he pulled the strap on the elevator door.

Eddie, panicked, said, "Thanks for everything, Aunt Lily," which wasn't exactly the same as "I love you" but would have to do because Aunt Lily's touchy-feeliness made Eddie really uncomfortable.

On the street, Alex said, "We won't go to Melville's today, but the cutest girl works there, which is why I really like to go there. She's nineteen, so I don't actually have a hope in hell, and I think she might have a boyfriend, but I don't care."

"Uh, okay."

"Hey, don't be nervous. Everybody at school is really—well, I don't want to say nice, but definitely cool."

"I'm not nervous," Eddie lied.

"Don't worry. I was terrified before my first day last year. I was pissed about having to wear a tie every day. I really let Mom and Dad have it—you know, you guys got to go to normal schools, why am I such a freak that I have to go to the experimental school? But once I got there, I really liked it. I don't know—I see high schools on TV, and I'm glad my school's the way it is. I mean, do they really have tons of teachers you don't know, and lines of lockers that the smaller kids get stuffed into, and jocks who beat up nerdy kids and stuff?"

Eddie thought for a minute. He tried to remember all the high school stuff he'd seen on TV. "I guess not that many people actually look like they're twenty-five, and the girls on TV are usually hotter than the ones in school, and nobody on TV has zits, but otherwise, yeah, that is pretty much what OHS was like."

"Wow." Alex paused. "Hey, speaking of zits, can you see the Zit That Ate Boston up here on my forehead, or is my hair covering it okay?"

Eddie thought that was kind of a girlish thing to ask, but Alex had girlfriends, so maybe he knew stuff. "Uh, I can't see any zits."

"Cool."

They waited in silence at a stop until a Silver Line bus came by. Alex ran his pass through and Eddie dropped change into the box. They got off the bus downtown. People dressed much like Eddie and Alex were bustling around everywhere, heading into all these buildings, lining up at Melville's for coffee. Eddie did have to admit that it felt kind of cool to be one of these people, bustling down the street heading for an office tower, instead of standing on blacktop waiting for the bell to ring so he could squish through the halls.

Eddie watched, mystified, as Alex slapped the closing elevator doors and the grumpy old security guard looked up from his *Boston Herald* long enough to yell at him. What would make you want to wait till the doors were closing just to make them open again? It seemed like a dumb waste of time to Eddie, but he didn't say anything.

They were on the elevator for about a second, and then they came to the glass doors, and Alex swiped his card. "We'll make sure to go to Human Resources — that's the corny 'official business world' name for the office — and get you an ID today," Alex said.

They walked through the door, and Eddie just couldn't believe what he saw. The floor was covered in carpet. The walls had art on them. Real art, in frames with glass, not a bunch of crappy self-portraits from Mr. Benson's art class. The doors were big and heavy and made of real wood. There was no glass with the metal mesh inside it that was everywhere at OHS. There were no lockers. Mostly Eddie just couldn't believe what good shape everything was in. Nothing was tagged like it was at OHS, and it didn't look like anybody had tried to break anything on purpose. Everything looked nice and new. It even smelled good in here — kind of like oranges, and not like the ammonia they used to mop the hallways at OHS.

"Okay, here we are, Room 212, where all the magic happens," Alex said, pulling on the door. As it opened, a paper airplane came flying out and hit Eddie in the left eye.

"Ow, shit!" Eddie said, and clamped his jaw shut. He didn't know it, but his ears were turning red. The airplane in the eye hurt, but more than that, Eddie couldn't believe that he'd started life at a new school by swearing. He hoped he wouldn't get in trouble on his first day, though that would just about fit with the way the rest of his life was going.

"Oh, shoot, my b!" Kelvin called out. "Damn, you okay?"

Eddie rubbed his left eye. "Yeah, yeah, fine."

"Kelvin," Alex said, "this is my cousin Eddie."

"What's up?" Kelvin asked, standing up and extending his hand. Wow. This kid was really tall. Eddie wondered for a second if it would be racist to ask if he played basketball. Probably. Eddie reached his hand out to shake, and found Kelvin grabbing his hand in a way he'd seen on MTV but had never actually done himself. Eddie hoped he wouldn't have to lean back and fold his arms and hold three fingers up or something, because there was no way he was going to be able to do that right.

As it was, he barely managed to fake his way through the fist bump with Kelvin, and then he had to do it again with Savon. Eddie wondered if Savon knew his name meant "soap" in French, or if Kelvin was named after the temperature scale from science class. Eddie had never been popular in school, but he knew enough not to ask those questions.

Alex introduced him to Tanya, who was the only other white person in the room besides him and Alex, but who wore her hair all braided like the black girls, and then to Aisha, Gisela, Kenisha, and Hanh. Eddie was glad he didn't have to do weird handshakes with the girls, because that would have been embarrassing. They all just raised a hand, smiled, and went back to ignoring him, which was pretty much the treatment he was used to from girls.

What he wasn't used to, though, was the treatment he got from the boys. "So, Left Eye," Kelvin said, and everybody cracked up, and Eddie took his hand away from rubbing his left eye, which still really hurt from that paper airplane and was definitely watering and probably bloodshot. He noticed that Alex was trying hard not to laugh. "What's crackin'?"

"Uh, well . . ." Eddie wished he had a quick comeback, something nasty to say about Kelvin's aim with the paper airplane, something funny, anything at all . . .

"Okay, okay, quiet type, I get that, I get that. Yo, Alex, man, we figured your cousin would be white, but Left Eye is *literally* white! Can't see his face next to the wall!"

"Kid could be completely invisible in a snowstorm!" Savon added.

"Homeboy makes Michael Jackson look black!" Kelvin added, which brought laughter from the whole room.

"Hang on," Savon said, "I see something. Something . . . damn! Look at those red ears! Yo, Alex, your uncle a lobster or something, 'cause homeboy . . ." Eddie was glad to see that Alex looked shocked and horrified, but it wasn't enough to stop his anger.

"Alex's uncle is dead, and your name means 'soap,'" Eddie said, hating how stupid it sounded the minute it came out of his mouth. He'd killed whatever advantage he might have had from the dead-dad thing by trying to add the stupid French thing. He turned around to walk out, and Savon said, "Oh, yo, man, I'm sorry. I didn't know, I'm . . . sorry your dad passed."

"Yeah," Kelvin added, "Savon thinks just 'cause his dad's alive and locked up, everybody's is!"

"Shut up, Kelvin," Savon said. "My dad ain't in jail."

"That you know of. All I'm sayin'."

Alex finally piped up. "Damn, Kelvin. That wasn't right." Sure, he'd stick up for Soap, but not his own cousin.

Gisela said, "Y'all are out of control today. Where's the love, people? You"—she pointed to Savon—"didn't have to take it there, and you"—to Kelvin—"didn't have to take it there. Talking about people's fathers. Y'all got to leave family out of it."

"Yeah, okay, Your Highness," Kelvin said, but he shut up, and Eddie was glad Gisela stuck up for him.

Eddie was still standing next to the door, which opened and hit him in the back. A big-headed white guy with salt-and-pepper hair poked his head in. "Sorry about that, my young friend. Advisory 212! I am delighted to see so many of you here before the official start of the business day! You could certainly teach several of our fourth-year associates a lesson in punctuality."

"Well, Mr. Paulson, we need to get through that Dudley Square bus stop before the troublemakers get out of bed," Aisha said.

"Same thing at Forest Hills," Hanh offered. "You get there after eight, mad heads be hanging around trying to start something."

Paulson stopped smiling for a second, closed his eyes, and took a deep breath. He looked like he was actually in pain. "Young people, I am truly sorry on behalf of our city and our nation that you should have to think for even a second about whether your journey to school will be a safe one. All of us here at CUE understand the difficulties and sacrifices you make in order to secure the education you deserve, and we respect you for it."

Nobody said anything. It was a little strange the way Paulson got all serious and sad for a minute. Eddie felt like he should rush in to fill the silence, but what could he say—"I know what it's like, nobody went into the bathroom next to the third-floor science lab at my school unless they wanted to get beaten up"? Somehow it seemed different. And this was his school now anyway.

Pauslon's face cleared, and he said, "Having said all that, what have you been told about closing the conference room door?"

"I'm sorry, Mr. Paulson," Kelvin said, grinning. "We know that the other advisories like to get work done before school starts, and Kenisha's a little out of control."

Kenisha looked up from her book, adjusted her glasses, and said, "Mr. Paulson," but he cut her off.

"Please, Kelvin. The fact that Kenisha outscores you by ten points on everything does not make her out of control." This brought a chorus of "Oooohhs!" from the rest of the advisory, and a small smile from Kenisha as she returned to reading. "Now, Edward, my friend, you and I need to have a brief meeting before advisory gets under way, so you can get the lay of the land here at the finest school in America. If you don't mind accompanying me to my office . . ."

Eddie was happy for the opportunity to get out of the line of fire, but he was not too psyched to be heading to the principal's office. The principal at OHS never even knew his name, and he had liked it that way.

His first day of school hadn't even officially started yet, and already he'd been hit in the eye, insulted, and summoned to the principal's office. Terrific.

"Now, Edward, you're coming from Oldham, I believe?"

"Yes."

"Ah yes. I did some observations at OHS for my secondary administration certification. So the halls of the Center for Urban Education are probably looking very strange to you right now."

"Uh, yeah."

"You will note the lack of graffiti, and also, though the school day hasn't officially started yet, the lack of desks for hall monitors."

"So, um, do the hall monitors walk up and down the halls instead of sitting by the bathrooms?"

Paulson smiled. "No, Edward. We have no hall monitors here, and you will never be asked for a hall pass. We consider ourselves a community here, and, as such, we give each other freedom and expect responsibility. It's our assumption that you know where you need to be during the day and that you are responsible enough to be there. We assume that if you are on your way to the bathroom, you actually need to use the bathroom. We assume that when you leave the building for lunch, you will be able to return to class on time and not cause trouble on the streets. Now, the overwhelming majority of students thrive under such conditions. Some, of course, do not, but there is no need to treat the entire student body like criminals simply because a small percentage need extra help remembering their responsibilities."

This sounded like about the dumbest thing Eddie ever heard. This guy obviously knew nothing about teenagers. Eddie was sure kids walked all over him. Oh well. That was better than a mean principal any day, especially if the principal was actually going to know his name.

"And you've spent a few minutes in the advisory room?"

"Um. Yeah."

"I assume advisory is an unfamiliar concept to you as well?"

Eddie didn't quite know how to play this. Alex had told him how they had stupid names for everything here, and he figured advisory was just a dumb name for homeroom, but he knew if the principal was saying he assumed he didn't know something, he should act like he didn't know it.

"Um, yeah."

"Well, I'm sure Alex has explained it to you somewhat, but, in a nutshell, it's incredibly important in the business world and in life that people be able to work in teams. Now, simply because of the way scheduling works, we couldn't have you in the same classes all day with the same students, so we've created advisory as a way of grounding all students with a group. I'm sure you will find this 'corny,' as Kelvin likes to say, but we really view the advisory as a way of building a familylike atmosphere here. It really does become a tight-knit community. And, in addition, your advisor, Mr. Harrison, is your primary adult contact in this building. So when you or your guardians have questions, when you get report cards, when you have a

conflict that needs mediating, your advisor is there to help
you."

Great, Eddie thought. Somebody else breathing down his
neck, and more talking about family. My family's broken,
Eddie wanted to say, and I can do just fine by myself. I didn't
need an advisor at OHS, and that was a way bigger and
meaner school than this one. Paulson kept talking about freedom and responsibility, and about how you stayed in your advisory until you graduated, and how people really looked after
their advisory rooms, and Eddie just nodded and smiled and
tried to look interested. The only interesting thing that Paulson told him, though, was that Eddie should ask Alex about
what had happened when he'd left a potato chip bag on the
floor of an advisory of fourth-year associates last year.

6

AS SOON AS EDDIE WAS OUT THE
door, Alex decided he could stick up for him. He had a vague
sense that he probably should have stood up for him while he
was actually in the room, but he wasn't sure if Eddie would get
upset. It never looks good for a "young man," as Paulson
would call him, to have somebody else fight his battles. And
Eddie did need to learn how to take a joke and give one back.
It sure hadn't been easy for Alex to learn that. Still, Eddie was
family, and Alex owed him some loyalty.

"Gisela's right, you guys. Y'all were a little rough on him."

Kelvin immediately said, "Shoot, I was harder on Savon,
and he's my dawg." This was accompanied by a punch to
Savon's shoulder.

"Still."

"Aw, he knows we're playing. Doesn't he?" Kelvin asked.

"I really don't know, to be honest with you. Kid doesn't talk much."

"Maybe you should try to be more like him, Alex," Hanh called out.

"Maybe you ought to . . ." stop being so hot so I can pay attention in math class, part of Alex wanted to say, but instead he said, "try to act more like a normal Asian girl—be quiet for a minute and get some good math grades."

"Yeah, that's why you try to copy off my quizzes."

"That's a lie!"

"Yeah," Savon said, "Alex copies off me!"

"All I know is he's always staring over my shoulder in math class!"

"That's because he's trying to look down your shirt, genius! I thought Asians were supposed to be smart!" Kelvin retorted, and Alex knew he needed to come back with some crack about how there was nothing to see down Hanh's shirt or something, but he found that his mouth suddenly wasn't working. He held up his history book to hide his face because he was blushing so hard he was practically purple. He was going to kill Kelvin, who, of course, was right. Alex would never copy off Hanh when he sat next to Savon already, but Hanh was always "pushing the boundaries of professional attire," as Mr. Paulson called it, and so, yeah, he . . . ugh. Alex was dimly aware that the whole advisory was going "Oooh!" and laughing, and he wondered if Hanh was hiding, too; if she was embarrassed because she liked him, too.

Fortunately for Alex, Harrison entered at that moment.

"Damn, Harry," Kelvin said, "we were just about to really let Alex have it."

"Well," Harrison said, "there's so much wrong in that little sentence. First, you began it with a swear word—admittedly a mild swear word, but one that's clearly out of the CUE code of professional language—"

"That's the FA-CUE code of professional language," Alex piped up, sensing his opportunity to get out of the social hole he was in, and everybody laughed, definitely a good sign.

Harrison stopped talking and stared at Alex, visibly annoyed. Alex kept talking. "What? I mean, isn't this the Francis Abernathy Center for Urban Education? I mean, I'm just saying the name of the school over here—"

"Yeah, yeah, yeah. Well, yes, we can't possibly change the name as long as Abernathy is mayor, which looks like it'll be until all of your grandchildren die, but I feel like that joke is really, really tired. And, Kelvin, don't call me Harry, and don't even hint that there's anything going on in here before I get here, because if I have direct knowledge that something other than quiet study is taking place here before the official opening of school, then I will need to arrive earlier to supervise this time, like most other advisors do, as I'm sure you're aware. If, on the other hand, I believe you to be studying quietly in seats or making your way here prior to the official opening of school at 8:25, then I have no reason to arrive before, say, 8:20, and we can continue our fine current arrangement. Am I clear?"

"Yes, sir, Mr. Harrison sir!" Kelvin answered.

"That's more like it," Harrison said, trying and failing to

stop a smile. "About time I got the respect I deserve around here. Hey, Alex, where's your cousin? Isn't he starting today?"

"Yeah, he's talking to the chief executive officer, getting the professionalism lecture with a side order of 'freedom and responsibility.' "

"All right, then, well, let's try to make him feel welcome as soon as he arrives," Harrison said, and Gisela snorted.

By the time Eddie returned, it was transition time, and Harrison made everybody introduce themselves to him in professional language, even Alex, which was really dumb. He shared a bedroom with the kid, it wasn't like he needed to introduce himself. When it was Eddie's turn, he said, "Uh, my name is Eddie, which I guess you know. I was living in Oldham until recently." Alex's heart sank. Eddie had a great opportunity to make some joke about paper airplanes, or dis Kelvin in front of Harry without Harry noticing, but he didn't take it.

They had put Eddie in a different English class from his, so Alex didn't see him again until marketing, which was this weird combination of an art, math, and English class that every sophomore at FA-CUE had to take. The marketing teacher, Mr. Lewis, was an old white guy who had worked in some company for his whole life and was trying to give back to the community or something. Everybody knew that nobody in any other school took a class like this, so it might have been easy to treat it like a joke if Lewis wasn't so serious and such a hard grader. On the first day he gave them this long lecture about marketing and how they were always on the receiving end, and how if they could understand it, this would be tremendously empowering. Alex didn't quite get the

speech, but apparently Lewis gave the same one at parents'
night, and Alex's mom and dad were completely in love with
him.

The other thing about Lewis was that he was really funny, if
you could figure out when he was making a joke. He said
everything totally seriously, but Alex had learned that Lewis
had a little twinkle in his eyes when he was joking, and he and
Savon were the only ones who ever laughed.

Eddie came into the room after Alex had found his usual
seat next to Savon. "Hey, Eddie, you can sit over here with
us—there are no assigned seats," Alex called to his cousin.

Eddie kept walking to the other end of the classroom and
sat by himself. "That's okay, you sit with your friends," he said,
obviously still pissed about that morning. Fine, Alex thought.
Be like that. Baby.

Lewis got up from his desk and walked over to the white-
board. The whole class fell silent. Alex had learned the hard
way that you didn't talk once Lewis got up from his desk.

"Today," Lewis said without even a hello or good morning or
anything, "is an auspicious day. It is a day that I am sure most
of you have been awaiting with bated breath, as I'm sure my
previous students have related to you the carnival of learning
fun that is the Marketing Project."

Alex winced. He'd been pretending that the Marketing
Project wasn't really going to happen this year, and here it
was. Whenever the Marketing Project came up, anybody who
had already done it just kind of shuddered and said something
along the lines of "Oh. That was *hard*." This never bothered
Alex so much, because older kids were always trying to scare

the classes behind them by telling them how hard everything was. What did scare him, though, was the fact that they would never say anything else about it. It wasn't like they wanted to talk it up to scare people; it was more like it was something so painful they couldn't stand to talk about it.

Lewis did his best to play up how scary the project was, explaining that it would test their math skills, their creativity, their ability to work with others, and their ability to do a great deal of work in a short period of time.

"Your first task will be an individual one," Lewis said. "I expect you to research a business that started no fewer than five and no more than thirty years ago."

That would probably include a whole lot of porn sites, Alex thought immediately. He daydreamed briefly about having a conversation in which he said something like "It's research for school, Mom, I swear!" and decided that he couldn't really do it, even though it was a funny idea.

"And before you ask, no, you may not research any company that purveys pornography over the Internet or, indeed, in any other format." A couple of people snickered, and Alex noticed that Lewis was looking right at him with that twinkly look in his eye. Scary. "Trace the business's development, and analyze what role marketing played in the ultimate success or failure of that business."

Alex looked over at Eddie. He had a notebook open and was writing down everything Lewis said. Actually, so were most people in the class. But Lewis always gave assignment sheets. Why did everybody waste their time doing way more work than they had to?

Lewis said some more stuff about how he wanted them to write a proposal for the project, and then he handed out the assignment sheet, just as Alex knew he would.

When marketing ended, Alex tried to catch up to Eddie, but he disappeared into the hallway before Alex even had all his stuff packed up.

Even though Alex knew that Eddie had overreacted this morning, he did feel a little bad, and so he was glad when he found Eddie at the end of the day. "Hey! How did your day go?" he asked.

"Okay, I guess."

"So, uh, did you meet anybody else?"

"You know, I kinda kept to myself today, after this morning."

"Yeah, well, those guys can be kinda rough, you know, but it really is all in fun."

"Sure." Eddie didn't sound convinced, or at least he seemed to be saying that it wasn't that fun for him. Well, tough. Alex didn't know what school was like for Eddie before, but CUE was where he was now, so he'd better get used to it.

But, as his first day turned into his first week, and started moving toward his first month, Eddie didn't get used to it. Or, anyway, he only got used to part of it. He always had his homework complete, and he aced the first history test even though he'd missed the first week of the unit. Eddie was pretty much a study machine. Every day when they got home at about four-thirty, he would quietly watch CNN or ESPN for an hour, study until dinner, eat, and then go to their room and study. Eddie started his individual marketing project on ESPN before Alex had even really picked a company. Alex actually took his time picking a company, because the deadline seemed a long way away. This, of course, got the FA-CUE faculty into full FA-CUE mode, and Lewis talked to Harrison, Harrison took Alex aside, and then, two days later, called Mom and Dad, which meant no PlayStation until he got his work done. Alex spent the whole night typing up a proposal and asked Lewis the next day if he could do a product launch instead of a new company, and could he do his project on the PlayStation?

"Ah, a subject with which I am guessing you have a certain amount of familiarity. Indeed, if your advisor is to be believed, perhaps a little too much familiarity." Lewis smiled and approved the project, but Alex was pissed. Harrison had obviously reported back what Dad had said about PlayStation, and it wasn't like that was so private, but it was just incredibly annoying to have every adult in his life up in his business all the time.

Meanwhile, Eddie just kept on coming home every night, and watching exactly sixty minutes of television (Alex started looking at his watch and noticing that if Eddie started watching at 4:27, he turned the TV off at exactly 5:27). That seemed a little what Dad would call anal-retentive, but then again, if you looked at Eddie's grades, Alex guessed you couldn't really argue with the results.

Alex would start studying eventually, but not until he had thought about Hanh for a while, thought about Jennifer from his English class, thought about Marie also from English and history classes, played his daily thirty-minute allotment of PS2, watched his daily hour of television, and called at least two of his friends.

When they were at home, Eddie mostly studied, and even though he and Alex would talk, Alex didn't really feel like they were friends or anything. At least, not like Kelvin and Savon were. At school, Eddie didn't seem like he was still mad, but he also didn't fit in. He would study in advisory, just like Kenisha, and, like Kenisha, he was mostly left out of all the stuff that went on in advisory before Harrison got there, which was the number two reason for getting out of bed as far as Alex was concerned. (Number one was still seeing which girls would be pushing the boundaries of professional attire.) Everyone, even the girls, referred to him as Left Eye, and Eddie mostly ignored them when they did this, not understanding that they were trying to include him, not exclude him. He was excluding himself. Alex went back and forth between being angry at Eddie for what he saw as his stubbornness, and feeling bad for him. But what could he do?

Finally, after dinner one night, Alex's mom and dad cornered him after Eddie had gone to do his homework.

"So," Dad said, "how's Eddie doing at school?"

"Well, jeez, look at how much he studies! He's doing great! He aced the history test last week, and of course he's never lost any privileges around here. I gotta say I'm a little nervous for when progress reports come home, 'cause the kid is definitely going to make me look bad, and let me tell you that I have some mixed feelings about that."

"Yeah, he obviously studies a lot," Dad said, "but that's not what we're talking about."

"Which I'm sure you know," Mom said, starting the parental tag-team maneuver. Alex hated it when they ran the tag team on him. He kind of wished he and Eddie were in trouble together, so that he could tag-team his parents for once, but Eddie did not look much like he was going to get in trouble, and this friendly-family-chat-while-we-clean-up-from-dinner was suddenly smelling a lot like Alex Gets Yelled At.

"It's just," Mom said, "this has to be difficult for him, socially, not knowing anybody here, and we're just concerned that you're not doing—"

"That," Dad continued, making sure Alex couldn't get a word in while Mom paused for breath, "you're afraid of looking like a dork in front of your friends, and that you're not doing all you should be to include him."

Now Alex was mad. "I am too doing everything I can! I can't make the kid be social! He comes in to advisory every day and puts his nose in a book! He doesn't talk to anybody in class except for the teacher! What am I supposed to do? If he doesn't want to talk I can't really make him. Hell, he barely talks to me! You guys are always trying to make him go grocery shopping or go with you to get the oil changed or whatever. Does he talk to you?"

"Yes, he does," said Mom, who apparently was Good Cop tonight, "but, as you are well aware, it's important for him to talk to his peers, too. We know that you can't make him talk to anyone, but you could try to include him in your activities."

"Look, you scared him out of going to Melville's with me, I can never find him at lunch anyway, and, I gotta be honest here, the kid is not a ton of fun to hang out with! It's impossible to talk to him without making him mad and turning his ears red, so it's not like you can have a normal conversation when he's around."

"If he's feeling awkward, that's understandable," Dad said. "But you have a responsibility to him that we feel you're not fulfilling. Mom and I are providing the house and the food and the stable adult presences and we're doing everything we can to include him socially in all of our family activities, but we can't do anything about his peer group, and that is something that you have a familial obligation to help him with."

Alex slammed down a dish and surprised himself by yelling, "The kid is fifteen years old! I can't make him talk to anybody, which I already told you if you were listening, which you weren't, as usual! I can't make somebody popular, okay? I swear to God this is so unfair! You don't have any idea what goes on at school, and you accuse me of not trying. You know what, forget it, I'm a horrible person, so go ahead and punish me or whatever, but right now I'm going to go study." And with that, he walked out.

Parents were so stupid. Like he could do anything for Eddie when Eddie wouldn't do anything for himself. Honestly. Alex glared at Eddie, hunched over his history book, when he got into the room, but Eddie didn't even notice.

Alex went to bed angry without saying good night to his parents or Eddie. To hell with all of them.

The next day in advisory, Alex kind of stepped outside himself for a minute and noticed that he was spending all his time talking to people besides Eddie. And yeah, Eddie wasn't very social, but Alex realized guiltily that he had given up on him— he had basically stopped trying to talk to him in advisory after about the second day. So maybe there was more he could do, and that pissed him off, because while Mom and Dad were being so unfair, they were also kind of right.

7

AFTER HIS DISASTROUS FIRST DAY,
Eddie decided to just keep his head down and his grades up
and not pay attention to anything else. He knew that Alex's
friends were still calling him Left Eye, but it stopped bother-
ing him. He would just concentrate on schoolwork until Mom
got out of rehab. That wouldn't be so long, and even though
he didn't have any friends, he had to admit that his life here
was actually a little better than it had been at home.

For one thing, school went until four, so he didn't have to
sign up for a lot of activities to keep busy. Which was good,
because CUE didn't really have any activities. Also, it was
okay to be smart here, which was certainly a new experience
for Eddie. There wasn't the constant danger that somebody
was going to beat you up for messing up the curve or whatever. And being one of the few white kids turned out to be no

problem at all outside of the 212 advisory. If anything, it seemed to give most people an extra reason to leave him alone. He didn't ever really feel like he stuck out—he just felt like he was basically invisible. And this suited him fine.

Of course, Aunt Lily and Uncle Brian were always trying to get him to talk about it. They would invite him along on some errand or something, and he never felt like he could say no, even though who the hell wanted to go to the art supply store with Uncle Brian and buy canvas? And things would always be fine. Aunt Lily was nice, and Uncle Brian was really funny— you could tell that he was a lot like Alex but had to try to behave for Aunt Lily, so he was actually a lot of fun when he was by himself. But then they always spoiled it. At some point they would be like "So, how are you doing?" or "Have you heard anything from your mom?" or "You seem to be coping really well, you're a tough kid," and it was all Eddie could do to stop himself from yelling that they'd just ruined a perfectly good shopping trip or whatever.

And then there was the therapy. The therapist was this guy Don with curly graying hair and a big bushy graying mustache, and Eddie thought he was nice enough, but he couldn't see the point. He would talk, because otherwise you just had to sit there for an hour, which was uncomfortable, and then he would end up crying, and after he'd cried for most of the hour, he would usually feel worse than he felt before he went in. And then he'd feel like crap all night, and while on Tuesday night he would be thinking about ESPN and reading some article about their commercials, on Wednesday night after

therapy it was practically impossible to get any work done because he felt like he'd been beaten up. He didn't get how this
was supposed to be helping him.

Still, Aunt Lily and Uncle Brian picked out and paid for the
groceries, and Eddie only had to clean up one night out of
every three, and he didn't have to take care of the whole
house like he used to. Aunt Lily even did his laundry for him.
He literally almost cried the first time he found a pile of his
clothes all folded up on his bed, but he thought that crying
about laundry was just too wussy, so he stopped. He had
thought that doing everything for himself was kind of an ad-
venture at first, but now that he didn't have to do it and could
act as much like a normal teenager as a kid with a dead dad
and druggie mom could, he found that he felt a lot lighter and
he slept a lot better.

So Eddie was doing okay, which was all he ever told Aunt
Lily and Uncle Brian whenever they asked him annoying questions. He did wish he had some friends, or even a girlfriend,
or, let's face it, any fun at all, but he had decided long ago that
that kind of stuff would probably have to wait until college,
when he'd get a scholarship to someplace far away and meet
girls and go to parties and live in apartments in the summer
and work at a bookstore on campus and never have to see his
mom again.

But college was still a long way off. Right around the corner,
though, was a "half" day, which meant that school got out at a
normal time instead of four o'clock, and Eddie didn't know
what he would do. This was the problem with not having any
life outside of school. Eddie didn't even want to think about

spring break coming up in March, and how he would possibly fill his time without school when that rolled around. He wondered if normal kids dreaded vacation. He didn't think so. But Eddie was not a normal kid, and it was pointless to dwell on it.

Of course, knowing it was pointless didn't stop him from thinking about it all the time.

In some way, he wished Alex had done more to include him, or had been somebody he really liked hanging out with. Eddie tried to imagine a life where he had two parents who were alive and not obviously addicted to anything, and a bunch of friends he could laugh with all the time, and whether he'd want to risk losing his popularity if his study-buddy cousin showed up. He knew how that worked. Everybody knew if they invited you, you were going to have to bring the kid who was no fun, and pretty soon they stopped inviting you. At least, that was how it worked on TV. He didn't think he would take that hit for the team if he were in Alex's shoes, so he couldn't really blame Alex too much.

So Eddie was shocked on the way to the bus on the morning of the half day when Alex said, "Uh, I'm going over to Kelvin's after school. He's got the new Madden. You wanna come?"

Eddie thought about it. Madden. Madden was what he used to play with his dad, and the game he'd played more than any other in the two years since Dad died. He would spend days at a time taking some scrub team to the Super Bowl. So it reminded him of Dad, which was good, but of course also bad, but it also reminded him of the last year when Mom went from bad to worse, and that was just bad without being good at all. Not to mention the fact that all of Alex's friends obviously thought he was this white geek and they would probably be picking on him all afternoon.

But he was ahead in all his homework, and he hated the book they were reading in English. What else did he have to do? Maybe they'd even get to like him because they could pick on him. That happened on TV and in movies sometimes.

Of course, he had heard the big fight Alex had with his parents the other night, because the walls that Uncle Brian had famously framed up were really not that great for keeping the sound out. So he knew that Aunt Lily and Uncle Brian were concerned about him, which he thought was nice but also annoying, and now they had guilted Alex into inviting him to something. That made him mad because he thought Alex had been right that he was fifteen and could take care of himself; after all, he had basically been his own parent for at least a year and a half. It also made him mad that he was somebody that people took pity on, like he was some lost puppy or something. He knew he kind of was a lost puppy, and that made him mad, too.

But he thought about how he took the Cincinnati Bengals to the Super Bowl on Madden 2002, and he thought about sitting alone in the loft all afternoon, and he decided, what the hell. He wished he weren't a pathetic puppy, but he was, so there was no point in wishing things could be different.

"Yeah, okay," he said, and he saw Alex's shoulders slump down and relax.

Eddie's first half day at FA-CUE (which he always called it in his mind, because he did think it was pretty funny) was another in a long list of surprises about this weird school. Half days at OHS were a total joke—they had a movie in English class, a game in math, a movie in history, and that was usually it.

Here, though, they just acted like it was a regular day—his history teacher's lecture gave him four pages of notes, they had an in-class essay in English, and they started a new unit in math. Weird.

Finally Mr. Paulson, the "CEO," came over the P.A. system: "Greetings! As your supervisor, it is my pleasure to announce that the free afternoon for first-, second-, third-, and fourth-year associates begins now." Eddie waited for the loud whooping that would always accompany such an announcement at OHS, but none came. People just started quietly folding up their books and notebooks. "All partners"—this was FA-CUE speak for teachers—"will convene in Conference Room 315. Thank you for your attention, and have a productive afternoon." Productive. Like it would kill the guy to say "nice."

Eddie wandered into the hall, hoping he didn't have to stand there for twenty minutes feeling more and more like a loser until it became clear that Alex had ditched him.

As it turned out, it didn't happen that way, because as he was walking down the hall, a hand grabbed his elbow and spun him around. His first thought was that this was where the new kid has to get into a fight, which was a pretty common scene at OHS.

He felt silly immediately when he saw Savon smiling at him. "See, now you can't be loitering around on an early release day. You just got to get out as soon as possible. Think of it like a fire drill. Come on," Savon said, pulling Eddie toward the front doors.

"But, uh, why? I mean, what happens if you take five minutes to go to the bathroom and stuff?"

"Okay, it's like this," Savon said as he pulled Eddie into the stairwell so they could avoid the wait for the one elevator, which already had twenty people clustered around it. "You want to spend an afternoon listening to Paulson?"

Eddie thought about that. Paulson was nice enough, but even hanging out by himself all afternoon would be better than listening to Paulson go on and on about the best school in the world, blah blah blah.

"Uh, no," Eddie said.

"See, now neither do the teachers. And you've heard Paulson talking about 'Helping students is always our number one priority.' So a teacher sees you after school on a half day, they know you're a higher priority than the meeting, so all the sudden it's 'Why don't you make up that test you missed,' or 'I'm concerned about you, you need some extra help,' or 'Let's talk about your college choices,' or any damn thing they can think of so they can kill an hour with you instead of listening to Paulson. That's why you gotta be careful after school, man. Them teachers are desperate to get out of those meetings. They're like vultures, so you gotta move quick before they grab you."

If Eddie'd known that it was an option to stay after school and talk to a teacher instead of going to some probably dangerous neighborhood to get made fun of, he might just have done that. But oh well. Savon, anyway, was being nice to him today. Maybe, he thought, it was the fact that they were both short and they both studied and got good grades. It was kind of funny, because he actually had more in common with Savon than he did with Alex, if he thought about it.

They emerged in the lobby and found Alex and Kelvin waiting. "All right, finally!" Kelvin said. "Alex, man, you gotta tell Left Eye to move on a half day! Family gotta look out for each other. Homeboy could have been stuck with Mr. Weiskopf all afternoon!"

Mr. Weiskopf was the Spanish teacher. Mr. Ramirez was teaching them about Germany in World War I. Nobody but Eddie seemed to think this was odd.

"Yeah, you're right," Alex said. "Sorry, dawg," he said to Eddie, and Eddie thought it was weird the way Alex tried to talk half-black or something when he was at school, but not at home. But he did appreciate it. This was the most anybody at school had talked to him in weeks.

"That's okay," Eddie said. He wished he had a joke to make here, some way to dis Alex and show that he wasn't just a pathetic puppy target, but he couldn't think of anything.

"All right, let's go," Kelvin said, and they all headed toward the T stop. There was some other kid there, a black kid who Eddie had seen around school but didn't know. "This my little brother Deshawn. He's a first-year associate," Savon said. Eddie looked at Deshawn. He was about three inches taller than Savon. Now that's gotta suck, Eddie thought, and sure enough, Deshawn piped up with "Naw, see, I'm younger, but *you* the little one."

Savon acted like he hadn't heard. "Now see, Left Eye," he

said, "you gonna get to see some serious ghetto today. Serious ghetto."

"I don't know why you talking about ghetto," Kelvin answered. "You live across the street from the projects. Bullet holes all in the windows, people peeing in the doorway, and your moms on the sidewalk talking about do you wanna date?"

"Okay, okay, we'll see when we get to your house, if we make it there alive and the crackheads ain't stolen your PS2 yet."

"Damn, Savon," Deshawn said, "don't talk about Kelvin's parents like that." Everybody but Eddie laughed at this one, and as Savon said, "Oh, my fault, K, I know your parents ain't crackheads. They just got them nasty teeth . . ." Eddie wondered if any of these kids knew that somebody here actually did have a crackhead for a parent, or, anyway, a drug addict. Well, Alex obviously knew, and Eddie was glad that he just played along with the joke and didn't try to tell people, "Yo, don't talk about that around Eddie, dawg," or anything like that. Still, he hated the fact that his real life was the kind of thing normal kids, or even Alex's friends, laughed about.

Hey, he'd just made a joke! Only in his mind, but still. Maybe there was hope.

The T ride to Kelvin's house took forever. They took the Red Line to Ashmont, then changed to the Mattapan High Speed Trolley, which looked like something you'd see in an old black-and-white movie on cable, where the guys wore suits and hats all the time and said things like "Say, whaddya lookin' at, Mac? She's my gal, see?" The trolley clunked along at a speed that was not high, and Eddie noticed that he and Alex were the only white people on it. He also noticed that all the smiling and goofing this crew usually did stopped immediately when they got on the trolley. Everybody sat with their legs spread wide apart and stared into space like they were pissed off at somebody, or maybe just the world. Eddie did the same thing, and found that it was pretty easy.

Finally they got off and walked up the street to Kelvin's house. Eddie looked around, kind of surprised. Mattapan was on the news all the time—this was one of those mysterious places, Dorchester and Roxbury were the others—where people got shot, where Eddie pictured life as being like one long rap video. So, yes, he was kind of surprised to see nobody toting guns or dealing drugs. Kelvin's street was quiet and lined with triple-decker houses. Other than the two old ladies shuffling down the street, they didn't see anybody.

After Savon's intro, Eddie fully expected them to go into the triple-decker house with the peeling paint and the second-floor front porch that looked like it was about to fall down, but they walked right past this and went into the house three doors down. It was also a triple-decker, but the porches were straight and looked like they might actually hold the weight of somebody who stepped onto them, and the paint was not new but not peeling. Eddie was actually surprised at how normal it looked.

He was even more surprised when they got up into Kelvin's apartment on the third floor. He wasn't sure what he had been expecting—a big-screen TV and some ugly furniture, pictures of Jesus or Tupac hanging up somewhere, or maybe just filth. But Kelvin's apartment was clean and neat, and the living room looked a lot more normal than the one at Alex's house. Kelvin had a regular couch instead of that uncomfortable black thing with the chrome everywhere that was in Alex's living room, or anyway the part of the loft that they watched TV in. The TV was like the one in Eddie's old house instead of tiny like at Alex's, and the stuff on the wall was just paintings and family pictures, and the paintings were a lot more normal than Uncle Brian's paintings, especially that one that didn't really look like anything that Alex told him was called *Blue Vagina #6*.

Kelvin disappeared into the kitchen and returned with bowls of chips and pretzels and a couple of two-liter bottles of soda while Savon made himself at home and turned on the PS2 and the TV.

Since this was the brand-new Madden, they watched the whole intro, which they would never watch again. And then Kelvin said, "All right, so why don't Deshawn and Left Eye get the first game, and then, you know, the real competition can begin."

Ahhh. Now Eddie understood why Savon had been so nice to him, had wanted to make sure that he didn't get stuck talking to a teacher for an hour. He was looking out for his brother, trying to make sure Deshawn had somebody to beat. Well, he was in for a surprise.

"I got the Patriots!" Deshawn said, and Eddie just smiled. He knew from when Dad was alive that whoever didn't trust his own skills always picked the best team.

"Detroit Lions," Eddie said, and everyone snickered.

"Damn," Alex said, "Pats versus Lions. This is going to be

ugly." Oh, it was going to be ugly all right, but not the way
Alex thought. The game started, and Eddie quickly found
that Deshawn was terrible. After three plays on either side of
the ball, Eddie could read him like a book. He anticipated
pretty much every play Deshawn tried to run, so he stopped
his runs, intercepted his passes, and basically scored at will.
The final score was Detroit 42, New England 6.

He wanted very badly to talk trash, but he couldn't think of
any clever put-downs, and anyway he'd only just met Deshawn, so all he said was "Next!"

Apparently this was trashy enough, because it drew an
"Oh!" from somebody in the room. Eddie didn't know who,
because he didn't take his eyes off the screen.

"Okay, Alex," Kelvin said, "handle your cousin so I can handle you."

Alex smiled at Eddie kind of apologetically, as if to say,
"Yeah, sorry I have to do this to you, cousin." Well, he'd see.

And he did. Detroit 28, Tampa Bay 14.

Eddie was starting to get into that zone he sometimes used
to get into at 1 a.m. when he'd been playing all night and he
just felt like he couldn't possibly lose, and that was good because as soon as he went to bed, he'd be back in the real world.

Since Alex was family and Eddie was getting kind of buzzed
on adrenaline and the soda, he said, "Looks like the new kid
has some surprises up his sleeve. Who else wants some?"

This provoked grins from everyone, even Alex, who seemed
to be taking losing pretty well. Actually, Eddie thought, much
better than he himself would have.

"Okay, then, son," Kelvin said. "School's in."

"I don't know, Kel," Alex said, "I think this might be Left Eye's day." Eddie smiled. His dumb nickname didn't sound quite as dumb now that it was his day, and it was kind of nice to feel like Alex had his back, as they said at school.

Now Eddie didn't have to talk trash, because Savon and Alex, who were better at it anyway, kept up a steady patter at Kelvin. "Oh, you in trouble now, Kel," "Left Eye's got you on the ropes, homes," and stuff like that. This game was much closer than the other two, but even when Kelvin beat Eddie's defense and scored, Eddie was never worried. He knew he was going to win. And so he did: Detroit 28, Kansas City 21.

"Yeah! Who went to school? Who went to school? 'Cause I don't think it was me!" Eddie realized after the words were already out of his mouth that he'd never imagined saying something like that to a black kid who was like a yard taller than him and probably outweighed him by fifty pounds. Kelvin sulked while Alex, Deshawn, and Savon pointed at him and laughed.

"Oh!" Savon said. "In your own house, too. Homeboy came into your house and chumped you right there on your own couch!"

Savon then wiped the grin off his face, got a real serious expression, and stepped up to the controller. "Okay, Left Eye," he said, "you had a good run, and I appreciate you puttin' Kelvin in his place, but now you're done."

"We'll see about that, Soap," Eddie said.

"Soap again? What the hell is that?" Kelvin laughed. "That some kinda white boy suburban cap or something? You really hate somebody you call 'em detergent? What the hell is soap?"

"Soap!" Eddie replied, then watched as some stranger who appeared to be in control of his mouth said, "The kid's name means soap in French! Look it up!"

Kelvin looked quizzically at him, then went and started up his computer. As Eddie's Detroit Lions received the opening kickoff from Savon's New Orleans Saints (Eddie knew that Savon's choice of team silently showed him respect. Savon was already planning for the possibility of his defeat by picking a team almost as bad as the Lions so he wouldn't have the added humiliation of having lost with a better team), Kelvin called out, "He's right! *Savon* means 'soap'!"

This caused some laughs, which Eddie observed did not disturb Savon at all. The game was much tougher than any of the others from the beginning. Defenses dominated, and neither team seemed able to score. Kelvin and Alex cheered Eddie on, while Deshawn rooted for Savon. Finally, as the clock wound down, Eddie completed a 20-yard pass to get him into field goal range and made the kick as time ran out. Detroit 10, New Orleans 7.

He'd beaten them all. He threw his controller down on the couch, jumped up, and watched again as the kid who looked just like him but said things he'd never even think of saying yelled out, "Woooooo! Yeah! How ya like me now, bitches? Huh?"

There was a moment of silence, and Eddie was suddenly terrified that he'd crossed some invisible line he hadn't even known was there. Savon, Alex, Kelvin, and Deshawn looked at each other in silence, and then simultaneously started laughing hysterically.

"He . . ." Kelvin laughed, "he . . . damn, he said that so white . . ." More laughter. "All 'How do you like me now, bitches?' "

Everybody continued to laugh, and Eddie started laughing, too, and found himself being punched in the shoulder in a friendly way, bumping fists, and hearing compliments about his Madden skills. He laughed and laughed, and he thought he might still be a pathetic puppy, but it was really nice, even just for a few minutes, to feel like a big dog.

8

EDDIE IMMEDIATELY BECAME MORE
bearable after their afternoon over at Kelvin's. Now when he
was greeted with "Yo, Left Eye!" in advisory, he'd come back
with "Soap! Temperature Scale! What up?" He'd had to explain the whole temperature scale thing, which took forever
and was not that funny but had something to do with absolute
zero, which Alex thought would be a much better nickname
for Kelvin than Temperature Scale.

Eddie was better at home, too. Alex could get him to play
Soul Caliber with him, and Eddie would actually laugh and
talk trash, even when he lost, which was often. It was like that
grumpy, quiet kid who used to live here was replaced by somebody who was actually kind of fun to hang out with. Alex still
wasn't crazy about sharing his space, but he had to admit it
was nice to have another kid here. Not only did he have somebody to joke with and ask for the homework he hadn't written

down, but since Eddie had some issues, it distracted Mom and Dad from crawling up Alex's butt about his grades all the time.

Of course, Eddie was still studying more than Alex was, and when progress reports came home, all of Eddie's mid-quarter grades were higher than Alex's. Lewis even singled Eddie out in class and talked about how his analysis of ESPN's success was a great example of how this project was supposed to be done, and everybody else should peruse it if they wondered what a B+ paper looked like, since most of them were quite far away from that territory and they would need to do much better on the group project, which would be assigned shortly. Alex's PlayStation paper got a C–, which set off another lecture from Mom about limiting his college choices. Eddie was funny, though—when a couple of kids came up to him after class and actually wanted to see his paper, he looked like he was about to fall over in shock. "If this was my old school," Eddie said, "kids would be lining up to kick my ass after Mr. Lewis said that."

Overall, Alex thought Eddie's study studliness was kind of funny because they had had all these meetings with Paulson about how Eddie was going to have a difficult adjustment period, how the founders thought it was impossible for anyone unused to the academic rigor at CUE to adjust to it after the ninth grade, and how Eddie was the first transfer student in the history of the school. It turned out that Eddie had no trouble at all adjusting to the academic rigor, while Alex was still happy getting C's and B's.

Eddie got so comfortable that he even took on Gisela. One

day Eddie randomly piped up with, "Hey, you know, I was looking at the map, and actually, I mean, technically speaking, Cape Verde is not really *in* Africa." There was shocked silence in the advisory. Before this, Kelvin had been the only one dumb enough to challenge Gisela.

Gisela stood up to her entire six feet and loomed over Eddie, who, Alex had to give it to him, kept his cool and continued talking. "I mean, Cape Verde is a series of islands in the Atlantic Ocean, so when you say it's *in* Africa, I think it would really be more accurate to say it's *off the coast of* Africa, since it's several hundred miles to the African mainland."

"What state is Nantucket in?" was Gisela's only reply.

"Uh, well, that would be Massachusetts," Eddie said tentatively, and Alex knew he was done.

"Oh, so that is an island in the Atlantic Ocean, but according to you, it's in Massachusetts! What continent is Ireland part of? Do you know that? Do you know that the Republic of Ireland is part of the *European* Union? Oh! So it looks like that's another island in the Atlantic Ocean! But according to the European Union, it's part of Europe! Hmm, what about Great Britain? What continent is that part of? Oh, I see! What continent is the Philippines in? Hmm . . . I thought that was just a series of islands in the sea! So it looks like you got no idea what you're talking about, maybe you ought to do some more studying before you open your mouth, 'cause you got your head in those books every day and you obviously don't know anything!"

Alex looked sympathetically and somewhat nervously at Eddie, wondering if his ears would turn red and he'd start grinding his teeth again, but instead he just smiled and said, "Give me my dollar, Kelvin."

"What? What?" Gisela looked confused.

"Kelvin bet me a buck I wouldn't say anything to make you go off. Sorry. Nothing personal, I just kind of had to take the bet."

"Shoot, you taking a dollar from that fool? I'll give you five dollars if you get *him* to shut up for a whole day." Gisela smiled.

"Oh, see, she's just gotta stop being so in love with me. Talkin' about shut up and kiss me," Kelvin said, puckering up.

Gisela punched Kelvin hard on his upper arm, saying, "That's as close as you're ever gonna get to a kiss from me, big mouth."

Kelvin winced and said, "Damn, Gisela, that really hurt. See, now you just lucky you're female, because—"

"Because what? You wanna go? I'll take you down right here right in front of your boys. Yeah, you don't want that, all your boys see you cryin' like a little girl."

"Yeah, that would be almost as weird as *you* acting like a girl," Alex added, and Harrison, who seemed to have some kind of magical sense about this kind of stuff, came walking in just then and probably saved Alex's life.

So Eddie seemed to be getting used to life at Alex's house and at school. Well, except for Wednesday nights after he came back from his appointment. He usually went straight to their room, and sometimes Alex heard him punching the crap out of his futon, or sometimes it would be completely quiet in there. Alex felt bad—he wanted to help somehow, but he had no idea what would be the right thing to say, or even if there was anything to say. So he'd just hang out in the living room and feel kind of bad, thinking he could make it better if he only knew what the secret thing was to do.

One Wednesday night, when Eddie was in their room and Alex was on the couch with Dad, he said, "Why do you guys make him do this? It only seems to make it worse."

Dad looked sort of uncomfortable. "I guess the idea is that he's actually this upset every day, and we need to give him permission to feel it and not feel like he has to hold himself together all the time."

Alex thought that sounded nuts, but maybe his dad knew what he was talking about.

So apart from Wednesday nights, when he was worried about Eddie, Alex could devote some more energy to thinking about Hanh, who seemed to be avoiding him since Kelvin made that joke that was actually true about Alex trying to look down her shirt in math class. Alex figured that Hanh was ignoring him either because she liked him, too, or because she hated him. It could go either way, and there was no easy way to go up and say "Are you ignoring me because you like me, or are you just ignoring me?" Maybe he'd try to concentrate on Marie for a while.

One Thursday, Alex stayed after class for "extra help" in history, braving Ramirez's nasty coffee breath just because he knew Marie was going to be there making up the homework she missed when she was absent on Wednesday. He wondered if Marie would date a non-Haitian. He stared at her while Ramirez went on and on about the Treaty of Versailles, until

Ramirez busted him with "Alex, if you're just here to stare at Marie, I can stop talking and save myself some energy."

Busted again, and he could feel himself blushing. "Sorry, Mr. R. I was just thinking about how hard it must have been to live in postwar Germany under the provisions of this treaty." He wasn't sure Ramirez bought it, but he did keep talking for another twenty minutes.

When Alex got home that day, he was met by Eddie, who was on his way out, which Alex thought was kind of weird, since Eddie didn't really know the city very well, apart from their bus stop and the area right around school.

"Yo, Eddie, where you going?" he asked, but Eddie just kept walking and acted like he hadn't heard.

That's rude, Alex thought, and went upstairs. Dad was cooking dinner tonight, which Alex figured was a pretty good reason to leave the house, but he didn't think that was Eddie's problem.

"Hey," he asked his dad, "what's up with Eddie?"

"What do you mean?" Dad said as he tried to scoop something that Alex was really afraid was gross fennel into a frying pan while holding a cookbook in the other hand.

"Eddie? Kind of short kid, brown hair? Lives here?"

"Okay, smart-ass, okay. What do you mean what's up with him?" Dad stirred the substance, which now that Alex smelled it was definitely nasty fennel, in the sizzling pan and prepared to add some turkey sausage. Ecch.

"I mean, he just ran out of here and wouldn't answer me when I called after him."

"Oh. Wow. I had no idea he even left. I really don't know. Maybe you should go after him."

"I'll ask Mom. Where is she?"

"Laundry."

"Okay." Alex took the elevator to the basement and found his mom sitting on the dryer reading a book.

"Oh dear," she said when Alex told her that Eddie had stormed out. "I was afraid that might happen. He got a letter today."

"Yeah, I always run out of the house when I get a letter. What are you talking about, Mom?"

"It was from his mom. I got one, too. I guess Dinah's apologizing to everyone she harmed because of . . . well, you know. Her problem. His envelope was a lot fatter than mine."

"Whoa."

"Yeah, you'd better just give him some space for a while. He was pretty much raising himself before he came here according to Dinah's letter to me, so he can probably handle a few minutes on the city streets."

Alex took the elevator back upstairs and went into his room. On Eddie's bed was the letter from Aunt Dinah. Alex knew he shouldn't read it. But it was right there, and he would hear the elevator if Eddie came back, and it was pretty tempting.

No, Alex told himself, that would be wrong, and he wondered why his hands were picking the letter up anyway.

My dearest Eddie,

They've told me that one of the things I have to do in order to get better is to admit to myself and everybody else all the ways in which my addiction harmed them.

Well, you can see why I'm having a hard time figuring out where to start with you, ha-ha. (I know that's not really funny—I can tell by the way I'm crying as I write this.)

The last year is a blur to me, well actually the whole two-plus years since Dad died is a blur to me, and so I guess that's the first reason I should apologize. I didn't help you at all with how to live life without Dad. Instead I guess I pretty much stuck you with some brand-new problems.

Well, I suppose I stuck myself with some new problems, too. I guess I thought that the pills helped take Daddy's pain away, so maybe they can help take some of my pain away, too. And I really thought they were helping at first because they made me not care, and caring hurt so very much. But I was supposed to be the mom and be in charge of the house and take care of you, and soon I couldn't even take care of myself. I failed you, honey, I failed you really horribly, and I know you were worried. I do have some memories of those conversations before you gave up having them, when you were crying and telling me I had to stop. I wanted to, I really did, but I couldn't.

So far I'm doing a horrible job of this. Let me try this: I'm sorry you had to do all the grocery shopping because I was high or out. I'm sorry for every single time I yelled something horrible at you because I was drunk or high or because I wasn't drunk or high, and I can only remember some of those, Eddie, but I wish I couldn't remember any of them, sweetie, and I know this is probably hard to believe, but you are my own special sweetest boy and you always have been, and I never meant anything else I might have said. Oh, Eddie, I'm so sorry . . .

There were a lot more pages, but Alex suddenly felt kind of dirty for reading this. He carefully set the letter back on Eddie's bed, hoping it was in the same exact space where it had been, because he never wanted Eddie to know that he'd seen it.

Alex sat down on his own bed. He had known, of course, that Aunt Dinah was in rehab, and he figured it might have been kind of bad for Eddie, but it wasn't like Eddie ever talked about it or anything, and no matter what Dad said about giving him permission to be upset or whatever, Alex knew damn well that trying to get Eddie to talk about it would have been the wrong move, so he hadn't really known just how awful it had been.

Thinking about it made Alex want to cry. It also made him want to go hug his mom and tell her he loved her, and thank her for being his mom. It made him want to go hug his dad and say thanks, Dad, for staying alive and for cooking whatever horrible crap you are making for dinner.

But he couldn't really do that. Dad might die of shock. And anyway, he probably should find Eddie. No matter what Mom said, Alex didn't think Eddie was in the perfect shape to act sensible on the street, and if he walked about fifteen minutes in the wrong direction, he might find himself in some serious trouble. He tried to think like Eddie. Well, he'd probably stick to places he knew, even if he was really upset. Alex told his dad that he was going out to find Eddie, and did find himself saying "Thanks for cooking, Dad," as he passed through the kitchen. He ran to the elevator before Dad could get the stunned look off his face and ask him what that was all about.

9

EDDIE WAS RUNNING DOWN THE
street. He had no idea where he was running to, but pretty
soon his heart was pounding and he was breathing hard, and
that at least gave him something to think about besides the
fact that he wanted a different mom, a different self, a different life.

He couldn't stand it. First of all, Mom was bringing up stuff
she was sorry for that Eddie barely remembered, or anyway
that he had been trying not to think about, that he needed
not to think about if he was going to get through each day.
Second of all, the letter made him hate himself, made him
hate being Eddie, hate being Dinah's son, hate being the kid
that lived the life that the letter was about. He felt itchy and
jittery, and he knew that he had to get out of the loft.

He felt a little bad about ignoring Alex, but he also knew if
he opened his mouth, he'd start to cry, and he didn't want to

cry in front of Alex, who he suddenly hated for having his own alive parents who were weird, okay, but normal compared to Mom, because he knew how to talk to girls, because he had everything that Eddie didn't have.

After a few blocks he was totally out of breath, and he leaned up against a pole. Just then, a Silver Line bus pulled up, and Eddie decided to just get on, because why not—he had a bus pass and everything. The bus was pretty empty—not too many people going downtown at this hour, Eddie guessed. As he sat there, he thought about how he really wanted to do something crazy, something Eddie the goody-goody would never do, something that would get him outside of himself, even just for a little while.

He guessed a lot of teens who felt like he did right then probably started drinking or doing drugs or whatever, but Eddie saw what that got you, and he wasn't about to go down that road.

He got off at the usual stop because he didn't have any idea where else to go or what else to do. He saw the purple Melville's sign and decided to go in. He'd actually never even tried coffee—and right now that seemed like a good enough reason to go to a coffee shop.

It smelled nice inside, and there was some boring jazz playing slightly too loud. That girl that Alex was always pointing at through the window—Sheila, according to her nametag—was behind the counter and seemed to be the only person in the place. Eddie had to admit she was pretty cute. He looked at the menu over the counter. Coffee was the only word he really knew. Everything else was in a foreign language. What the hell was a caffè mocha? What was the difference between a cappuccino and a latte?

He stood there feeling stunned for a second, weighing whether to ask exactly what a cappuccino was, even though that was really embarrassing. He'd probably never come back here though, so he shouldn't care.

But then the music he hadn't even been paying attention to became something he couldn't ignore. He heard a little guitar intro and a xylophone or whatever it was ("It's a marimba!" Dad said in his mind), and even though it was just stupid hateful Elvis Costello singing "God's Comic" coming out of the speakers, it felt a lot more like a giant hand had just come out of the speakers and was squeezing his heart and trying to make it explode.

Dad had loved Elvis Costello, and Mom had listened to this awful song over and over and over after he died, and that was one more thing that pissed him off about Mom. Why would she want to keep hearing this song with the stupid dork going "Now I'm dead" over and over and over after Dad just died? Eddie had decided never to listen to or even mention Elvis Costello again, which turned out to be a pretty easy thing for a kid to do, because that was parent music anyway, so he had forgotten all about Elvis Costello and "God's Comic" until just now. And now on top of wanting to jump out of his skin because of Mom's letter, he missed Dad so much it actually hurt, and that led him back to everything that happened after Dad died, which led him back to the letter, which was the thing he was trying to run away from in the first place.

Sheila behind the counter looked at him and asked, "Are you okay?"

"I . . ." Eddie said, "this song . . . my dad . . ." and tears came spilling out of his eyes, and Sheila was asking, as Elvis Costello was saying "Now I'm dead" for the hundredth time, "Do you want me to change it?"

Eddie couldn't say anything, so he just nodded his head.

"I know how that goes. My dad used to listen to the Beatles and cry whenever he was drunk," Sheila said as she fiddled around with the CD changer behind the counter. Some other song that Eddie didn't know but which was sung by a lady and not Elvis Costello came on.

"My, um, my dad . . ." Eddie started to say, and then had to stop because he was crying again.

"Okay, okay," Sheila said. "You don't have to tell me. I didn't tell anybody anything for a long time, and I'm not always sure it helps anyway. Listen, let me get you something. You want a latte?"

Eddie didn't know what a latte was, but he nodded yes.

"Flavor shot? Vanilla?"

Eddie had no idea what she was talking about, but he just nodded again.

"Okay, go sit in the comfy chair there, grab a napkin or twelve, and I'll bring it out to you. It's on the house, or anyway, it's on my evil corporate masters."

Eddie slumped down in a big armchair, blew his nose, and tried to turn off the what-if machine in his mind. Because Dad did die, and Mom did lose it, and the life that Eddie had had with Mom and Dad in their happy little house was as dead as Dad was.

10

THE SUN HAD SET AND IT WAS
getting colder as Alex reached the street, and he looked up
and down trying to imagine where Eddie was. He walked
around the block and down a couple of the intersecting
streets and saw no sign of Eddie. Well, it wasn't like he and
Eddie ever spent much time walking around the South End.

He saw a Silver Line bus coming up Washington Street, and
he hopped on. Eddie seemed pretty happy at school, and the
guard would let him into the building as long as there was a
teacher in there, which there usually was in the early evening.

Alex rode ten minutes and got off right outside Melville's.
Reflexively he peeked inside to see if that cute girl with the
pink hair and the tattoo around her wrist was working, even
though she usually worked morning shifts. And yet there she
was, leaning over the counter to talk to somebody who was
sitting in one of those big chairs.

Alex reminded himself that he was supposed to be looking for Eddie, not scoping out the baristas, and he was about to turn and head toward FA-CUE when he saw that the customer with Sheila was Eddie.

Alex ran into Melville's and said, "Eddie! Mom and Dad are worried! What's going on, man?"

Eddie's eyes were all puffy and red, and he wiped his nose with a napkin and gave Alex a sad smile. "Oh, you know, the usual, a letter from my mom saying I'm so sorry, and reminding me of everything she's sorry about, and then some song my dead dad liked was on the stereo. No biggy. You want a latte?"

"It's on the house," Sheila said. "I'm moving to L.A. with my boyfriend tomorrow, so all coffee drinks are currently one hundred percent off." Boyfriend. Alex was right. Somehow that was worse than the fact that she was leaving town because it meant he couldn't even pretend he ever had a chance.

"In that case, make it a large, and gimme a hazelnut shot and some of those caramel droozles on the top," Alex said.

He called Dad while he waited for his latte, and he watched as Eddie sipped his latte deliberately. He told Dad that they were fine, and they would be home by seven-thirty at the latest. He added that they'd just grab a slice or something, and not to hold the fennel and organic turkey sausage concoction for them.

"So," Alex said as he sat down. He had no idea what to say, so all he said was "Sorry."

"Thanks. It's . . . I guess it's nice that she's getting better, but I was just starting to feel like this life was working out for me, you know, and I hate having to think about all that stuff, and then Dad and everything else."

"Yeah." They sipped their lattes in silence. Alex didn't have anything to say, so he just decided to keep his mouth shut rather than say some stupid thing about how he understood, he was here for him, dumb girly stuff that didn't really mean anything.

"Okay, Eddie," Sheila said. "Six-thirty, and I gotta close up here. I gotta be in the passenger seat of a Honda Civic at 5 a.m."

"Okay, Sheila. Thanks for the free coffee, and thanks for listening."

"No problem. Stay strong there, Ed. You're a tough kid. You'll be okay." All his Madden prowess aside, Alex didn't see Eddie as a tough kid, but thinking about what was in that letter, maybe he was.

Alex watched in shock as Sheila came out from behind the counter and gave Eddie a big hug. This was his first time in here! And Alex came in here like three times a week, and he barely got a hello!

"Uh, good luck in L.A.," Alex told Sheila as they left.

"Yeah, I figure they have coffee shops there, too, and no snow, so I'll be all set."

They walked out onto the dark street. "She lived in foster homes from the time she was fourteen," Eddie said. "She used to cut herself."

"Jesus, kid, you go out for one afternoon and you're the mack! You've got her life story and a hug! And the full-press hug, too!"

Eddie looked confused. "What the hell are you talking about?"

"The press! Like a lot of times if girls hug you, they kind of bend over at the waist and touch shoulders with you so that they won't press their boobs against you. But you got the full chest-to-chest, boobs-pressed-against-you hug!"

"Oh," Eddie said, "yeah, I guess. I didn't really notice." Alex said nothing and just stared at him. After a second, Eddie started laughing and said, "Well, okay, yeah, I did notice."

Alex smiled. "Dad was kind of worried about you. Mom said you'd be okay by yourself, but I figured I should check on you, you know, just to ease the old man's mind."

"Yeah, well, thanks. I mean, but, you know, I probably would have been okay. It's not like I know a lot of places to go."

"Here, I'll show you one," Alex said, and they walked up to the Downtown Crossing Orange Line station. Alex was a little unsure about sharing his favorite secret spot, but if anybody ever needed it, it seemed like Eddie did. Eddie wasn't crying or anything, but he might still be on the edge of losing it.

They got off at Back Bay and walked over to the library.

"The library? You go to the library? I honestly thought you were taking me to a porn store or something," Eddie said, smiling.

"Well, we could certainly go there later if you want, though this is actually mildly pornographic. But that's not why I like to come here." They walked in through the front door and went down a side hallway to a courtyard.

Alex opened the door to the courtyard, and they stepped out into the cold night. There were chairs and benches all around the outside of the square. The center was covered with some low green plants, and a naked lady made of bronze danced in the middle.

"So you see that there *is* a naked babe involved, but I like to come here when I want to think or whatever. It's peaceful, and pretty, and when it's not cold there's a fountain around her, which is nice, and nobody really bugs you unless you're trying to steal some homeless guy's seat or something."

They sat on a bench and looked at the statue in silence. Alex was about to suggest that they go grab a slice and head home, but as he looked over at Eddie, he saw that Eddie suddenly looked upset again.

"It's just . . ." Eddie said, and now he was crying, "it's like . . . she says she's sorry, but it's not that easy. She can't say she's sorry and expect it to be okay, because it's not okay. I wish she wasn't sorry, because then it would be easier to hate her, but now I feel like I should forgive her, but I can't because I hate her right now. I don't want to hate my mom, Alex."

"Yeah," Alex said, because he couldn't say "I know," because he didn't know. He didn't have any idea. I gave him the secret place, Alex thought. That's the best I can do.

11

EDDIE COULD TELL THAT ALEX really wanted to go home, and he should have said okay, let's go, I'm fine, but he wasn't fine. Even though it was really cold, he liked just sitting here, and he liked the look on the face of the naked statue lady. She looked like she had been covered in bronze right in the middle of the happiest moment of her life.

Finally Eddie's butt was frozen, and it was just too cold to stay out there any longer. Eddie didn't want to go home yet, because he still didn't know how he felt. For one thing, it wasn't *his* home; the letter had reminded him of that. He had been starting to think of Alex's house as his house or loft or whatever the hell it was, and he had started thinking of FA-CUE as his school, but now here was this letter from Mom, who was so sorry, and who did sound much better. Did that mean that she'd want him to go back to Oldham and OHS? He didn't want that life anymore. And he didn't want to hate her so much, especially when she was trying to be nice. Because then it was as if he, Eddie, the Kid Who Took Care of Himself for a Year and a Half, was the bad guy, when he was really the good guy here. Wasn't he?

"So, uh, I'm completely frozen. I guess we should grab a slice and then head home," Alex said, and Eddie knew he should say "Yeah," but instead he said, "I don't really feel like pizza. Is there someplace where we could just sit down for a while?"

"Well, there's a bunch of stuff in the mall, and some expensive yuppie restaurants on Newbury Street, or . . . I've got an idea. Let's go to Hanh's place!"

"You really like her, don't you?"

"She's okay," Alex said, but he was blushing, which wasn't something Eddie had believed Alex could do. "Her folks run Pho Saigon, and the food is totally awesome, and you get this gigantic bowl of noodle soup for around four bucks. And, yeah, if we happen to see Hanh there, that would be great. Come on, it's two stops away on the Orange Line."

Eddie found himself following Alex back to the Back Bay station, going to Chinatown at eight o'clock on a Thursday night to eat a bowl of Vietnamese soup so his cousin could scope out some girl. Even though his life had been pretty insane for more than a year, this seemed to him like the weirdest thing he'd ever done.

Eddie didn't say much—he was trying not to think about Mom's letter. Alex, on the other hand, seemed kind of nervous about seeing Hanh, and Eddie understood why. Alex could play off trying to look down her shirt because, let's face it, every guy in school did that, but there was really no way of playing off showing up at her family's restaurant.

"Playing it off" was a phrase he had learned at school. He tried to think about school—he still felt like the kids there were really Alex's friends. But they were people who actually talked to him, people he could lean over to when Tanya came into advisory looking really good and say, "Damn, she is looking *fine*."

Not that he had ever actually done that, but Savon had leaned over to him when Tanya walked in one morning and said, "Okay, Left Eye, see, you gotta close your mouth so the drool doesn't run out. 'Cause if she catches you looking, you're done, and if Kelvin notices you over here droolin', he's gonna blow up your spot all over this advisory." Eddie had to ask Alex later what "blowing up your spot" meant, but he got that it wasn't good. He was glad Savon had said something to him because it meant that he cared, sort of.

These were the things Eddie was thinking while Alex blabbed about "Boston's historic Chinatown, also known as the Combat Zone, don't worry, though, there wasn't any actual combat, it was because this is where all the prostitutes and porn stores were, before the same Francis Abernathy who gave his name to our fine school decided to clean things up down here."

And on and on and on he went. Eddie was actually kind of grateful, because he could kind of tune in to Alex's babbling whenever his mind tried to wander back to Mom, or Dad in his hospital bed—"I'm sorry I have to go, look out for your mom"—and he felt like screaming that he was so sorry, Dad, he screwed up, he couldn't look out for Mom, he couldn't hold everything together the way those kids did in every book they had to read in middle school where the dad or the pet or whatever dies and the kid Becomes a Man.

"Now as you no doubt noticed, there are still two or three porn stores down here, and of course there are still prostitutes down here, did you see those three back there? Not that I can personally imagine having sex with them even if they paid *me*, but just around this corner is the fabulous Pho Saigon, where the lovely Hanh may or may not be tonight but where we will most certainly enjoy the finest Pho in the greater Boston area, which sounds like something Paulson would say, but . . ." and Alex kept talking.

They reached Pho Saigon, which had a big red neon sign in the window. It looked like a cafeteria on the inside: white tile on the floor, red Formica booths. It did not, however, smell like any cafeteria Eddie had ever been in. School cafeterias always smelled like farts and disinfectant, and this place just smelled spicy and nice. The restaurant was about half-full, mostly with white guys who had big dreadlocks and metal barbells through their chins or else big beards that grew out of their necks, eating with their girlfriends, who looked like hippies but were at least kind of hot. Everybody in the place had a steaming gigantic bowl in front of them and expressions not unlike the statue lady's from the library.

Alex led Eddie to an empty table by the window, and they grabbed the menu from between a bottle of hot sauce and a napkin holder. The menu was in Vietnamese on one side, English on the other, but even the English side made no real sense to Eddie. "So, uh, what's good?" he asked Alex.

"The fact that I see Hanh back there, and she hasn't seen us yet," Alex said.

"Yeah, that's great, but I was actually—"

"Yeah, I know. Just get the pho with beef. It's really fantastic."

"Okay."

Hanh came over to the table holding an order pad. She looked at them, held back a smile, and said, "Oh no. Bad enough I have to see you guys every day, now you can't come in here and start talking trash."

"Nice to see you, too," Alex said. Just then his phone started to ring. He quickly hit a button to silence it. "I'm just trying to show my cousin here some of the culinary hot spots in Boston. Can we get two bowls of the pho with beef?"

"It's not 'foe,' dummy," Hanh said. "It's 'feuh?' "

"It does sound better that way," Alex said, "but it tastes great however you say it."

Hanh started to smile, then forced a frown and leaned way over their table, right in Alex's face, and whispered, "You'll be lucky if I don't spit in your soup. And if you start clowning me about anything in my family's restaurant in advisory tomorrow, I'm gonna kill you, even you, Left Eye, just for being related to this fool." And with that she walked away.

"She is so totally into me," Alex said, and Eddie couldn't help laughing.

Hanh brought their soup less than five minutes later, and

when she placed the bowls down in front of them, Alex quickly swapped them around. "Just in case," he said, smiling up at Hanh as he spooned some soup into his mouth.

"Joke's on you. I spat in both of 'em," Hanh said, but she was grinning this big grin, and Eddie figured, or at least hoped, she was joking. He spooned some of the soup into his mouth, and it was probably the oddest thing he had ever eaten. There were all kinds of spices going on at once, and some of them were kind of licorice-y, which was normally a taste that Eddie hated, but he took another spoonful, and he found that in this case, in this combination, he actually liked it a lot.

"Oh, wow," Eddie said. "I've never had anything like this. It's really good."

"Yeah, but don't say that too loud. I don't want Hanh to get a big head."

"See, I can hear you over there, and it would take a lot before my head got as big as your big ol' pumpkin head over there," Hanh yelled, and an older guy who Eddie figured was her dad yelled something at her in Vietnamese.

Alex blushed, smiled, and slurped.

Eddie was amazed at how much better he felt after eating. Nothing was different, really, except that he had a stomach full of delicious soup, but everything seemed different. He was in the city, and whatever happened with Mom, he was seeing new things and not trapped in his room alone in the old house in Oldham, and when you had a full stomach it was kind of amazing how much easier it was to believe that things were going to work out.

Of course, Dad was still dead, and he still had to go home and face the letter on his bed, but maybe he didn't have to face it alone.

Alex's phone rang again, and again he didn't answer it because he was talking to Hanh as he paid the check. As he approached Alex, he held up a piece of paper. "Digits, baby!" he said. "Life is looking good!"

12

ALEX WAS FEELING GREAT. HE HAD
been a good cousin and helped Eddie out. It was like he had
been trying for weeks to figure out what to do, and then he
just did it without thinking. And he had helped himself in the
process. He wasn't sure exactly what he would do now that he
had Hanh's cell phone number, but the point was that he had
the number, and she hadn't laughed at him or spit on him or
anything.

He felt so good that he totally forgot about their being two
hours late and about not answering his phone. He forgot, in
fact, to even worry for a second about Mom and Dad being
mad, because he'd done such a good thing, so when they
opened the elevator door and saw Mom and Dad standing
there with their tag-team game faces on, he froze.

"It's nine-thirty. Just where have you guys been?" Mom said, and Alex could see that Dad had staked out the Good Cop role this time, because he spoke calmly and slowly.

"Now, Alex, one of the things we spoke about when you got the phone was that you were going to need to be responsible about it, and that you would answer it when we called you. You told us you'd be home no later than seven-thirty. The two of you are out on the streets for two hours with us having no earthly idea where you are, why you're late, or what you're doing. We wouldn't have been mad about your being late if you'd only called. The phone was in your pocket, Alex. There's just no excuse."

"Anything could have happened!" Mom yelled. "What am I supposed to think when you won't answer your phone?"

Alex felt himself getting mad, and he was just on the verge of yelling that he had called, that they had to trust him a little bit, that he was sixteen years old, for God's sake, and that he could spend three and a half hours in the city he'd grown up in without having to talk to Mommy every five minutes.

Fortunately for Alex, Eddie stepped in with a lie so smooth Alex was actually jealous.

"I'm sorry, Aunt Lily, Uncle Brian," Eddie said. "It was really my fault. You know I got that letter from my mom telling me"—and he choked up a little bit, which Alex knew would help their case a lot—"telling me all the stuff she's sorry for. I was pretty upset, and so we were just walking around, and I guess I was telling him all about it." Alex watched as his parents' faces softened. Eddie was going to get them out of this!

"Anyway, we were talking and stuff, and I guess I got kind of

. . . I mean, Alex was being nice by not answering the phone while I was upset. I didn't even think that you'd be calling, because I guess I was too upset to think straight. I'm really sorry."

"It's okay, Eddie," Mom said. "I know how hard it is to read a letter like that. I got one, too." And she went over and hugged Eddie, and he hugged her back, and Alex could see tears welling up in both of their eyes.

"You still should have called," Dad said to Alex. "But it seems like you did a really good thing tonight. I'm proud of you."

"Thanks, Dad," Alex said, and he almost felt bad about Eddie lying them out of trouble, but then he thought, well, it was true that they had gone out to do something nice for Eddie, and so that was worth being proud of.

Later, in their room, Alex whispered, "Eddie, man, that was fantastic! Thanks for not saying anything about Hanh! You totally saved my butt! You're a really good liar!"

Eddie whispered, "When your mom's a drug addict, you get pretty good at lying. You know: my mom's not feeling well, she won't be able to make it to parents' night because she's working late, no, I'm not alone, my grandma is staying over, that kind of thing."

"Aw, I'm sorry."

"Don't be. Looks like it was good practice for hanging out with you." He smiled. "I had fun tonight."

"Me too."

"Yeah, you got a phone number."

"Hey, you got soup! And a full-press hug!"

"Yeah, from a girl who's leaving town. But it was excellent soup. Anyway, thanks."

"No problem," Alex said. He stayed awake thinking about Hanh, and, after a few minutes, he could hear Eddie crying softly in his bed.

The next day Alex and Eddie walked into advisory together. When Hanh arrived, she wouldn't look in their direction. Alex figured she was waiting to see if he would be a jerk and say something about last night, but he was keeping his mouth shut.

In fact, he decided to do the Eddie thing and just stick his nose in a book so that he didn't say anything stupid. Savon was doing the same thing, as were Eddie and, of course, Kenisha.

With this many people studying, and a big history test that afternoon, it got to be like a trend, and after five minutes everybody was studying. When Harrison arrived at eight-thirty, he looked around the room like something was wrong.

"Okay, what's going on?" he said. "Who had a fight? Where's Kelvin, and who hit him? Aisha?"

Aisha looked up from her math book. "Come on now, Harry, I got more sense than to get suspended because of *Kelvin.* You gotta give me some credit."

"And you gotta stop calling me Harry, but okay. So what's going on? You guys are so studious you must be up to something."

"Now see," Aisha piped up, "this is the kind of institutional racism we have to deal with. Room full of black kids is quiet, something must be wrong, somebody's sellin' crack in the back of the room."

Harrison was so easy to get this way, Alex thought it was almost unfair. Harrison got all flustered, and his face turned as red as his hair, and he started sputtering, "Now . . . listen, Aisha, I don't think it's fair to—"

"I don't think it's fair to call me a black kid!" Hanh said. Before he could think out whether it would look like he was defending Hanh, Alex added, "Yeah. See, that's the problem with being a minority in this school. We're just completely invisible to the majority culture!"

He and Hanh locked eyes for a minute, and then he looked away, hopefully before anybody noticed that they'd been looking at each other. Aisha and Gisela began to answer Alex at once, both yelling simultaneously.

"Well, Harry," Eddie added, "it sure isn't quiet now."

Eddie had never spoken to Mr. Harrison before, so now the entire advisory stared at him in awe. There was a moment of silence, and then gales of laughter, with Alex, Savon, and Gisela high-fiving Eddie and slapping him on the back.

"Okay, *now* he's a real member of advisory 212!" Gisela said.

Harrison just stood there with his mouth hanging open. Finally he said, "Well, this is great, I'm so pleased you guys have this wonderful bonding ritual. Make fun of the advisor, you're in. Do you remember that I'm writing college recommendations for you in a couple of years? You should start kissing up now if you want to get me to say anything nice at all." He delivered this whole speech like he sounded really tired, but he was smiling by the end of it. "Now, we actually do have a ton of stuff to talk about today because, as you may have heard, there was an incident of plagiarism. Fortunately, no one from this advisory was involved, but that means we need to have the plagiarism conversation yet again, so who'd like to open the floor with some comments?"

"Come on, Harry," Gisela said, "why do we have to have this conversation again just because Rodney gets caught copying because he's not as slick as certain students in the 212 advisory?"

Savon faked a fit that involved him coughing out "Alex" three or four times.

Harrison answered with "As long as plagiarism is a joke to you, we will keep talking about it. What you don't get is that it's not only wrong but can get you in huge trouble."

"So?" Gisela answered. "See, this is how this school is mad corny. Because you can't just talk to the kid who's in trouble, you have to talk to everybody. Right? I've never copied anybody's work in my life, because I got too much pride for that, but now I gotta listen to people lecturing me. Sorry, Mr. H., you know I love you, but you keep giving the boring lectures—and I'm doing what I'm supposed to do! It's like y'all think we're all guilty because one person does something stupid."

Harrison looked stumped. He was just about to muster a response when Kelvin came running through the door, panting.

"Yo, sorry, Harry! You know, my cousin got beef with some

dudes in Codman Square, so I can't take my normal bus, you know, I don't want to get shot for something my fool cousin did, so I had to *walk* all the way to Ashmont . . ."

"Shoot," Gisela said, "Ashmont got its own problems."

"Yeah," Kelvin said, "but I got no connection to either side of that beef, so it's cool for me."

"Yeah, cool for a dude," Aisha said, "but mad guys be hanging out there talking about 'Hey, shorty, what's your number?' and 'Why you gotta walk away like that?' I hate that place. That's why I take the bus all the way to Dudley."

Alex listened and said nothing. He was embarrassed because this was the city he thought Eddie had been expecting when he moved in. He also felt kind of weird because he lived in the same city as everybody else, but he could pretty much go where he wanted, and he never worried about who had beef with who.

Harrison was looking at his papers, and then he looked up and said, "Oh, Alex, can you step out with me for a second? I just have to go over some items with you."

Alex got embarrassed as everybody else in the room sent up a chorus of "Ooooohs." He walked into the hall with Harrison.

"So," Harrison said. "What do you think I want to talk to you about?"

Alex rolled his eyes and said in a bored voice, "My grades, how I'm not working up to my potential, stuff like that?"

Harrison looked stern, which was kind of weird, since he was usually so nice and friendly. "Are you bored with this conversation, Alex? Because I gotta be honest with you, I am, too. We talked around report card time, and you gave me some story about changes at your house, and how you were going to turn it around this quarter, and I'm getting the same e-mails from all your teachers that I always get—he's so smart, why doesn't he do better work?"

Alex looked at his shoes. Harrison's voice softened. "Look. I know you're tired of hearing this, but you're closing doors for yourself. You know what I mean? You can think of every C you get as another college that won't even look at you because of your GPA. You've just gotta start taking this stuff more seriously."

"Well, my dad failed a bunch of stuff in high school, and he had to do two years at community college before he could get into art school, and he did fine."

"Well, maybe you should ask him what he thinks. Because, I have to tell you, your dad is the one who always calls and e-mails me. He's worried about you, too. Maybe he wants you to have more choices than he did."

Alex didn't say anything. What was there to say? Girls are more interesting than history? Hell, Harry was a guy, he probably knew that. Should Alex admit that he never really felt like anything interested him? That answer never got you anything but "too bad" here at FA-CUE, which was suddenly what Alex felt like the whole school was saying to him.

The rest of the day went by as usual, though Alex was only dimly aware of anything that was happening because he was alternating between being mad at Harrison and, especially, Dad, and trying to figure out whether it would seem too desperate for him to call Hanh tonight, and what he should say if he did call her. The only other thing that did catch his attention was marketing class. "Well, up to now," Mr. Lewis said, "I've been laughably, indeed, almost negligently easy on you. I hope that my easy grading on the individual part of your project has not made you overconfident"—and Lewis was joking here, but if he thought he was going to get a smile out of Alex after he'd just gotten the lecture about why did you get a C–, he was completely insane—"for the group part of the project, which begins today."

Alex felt sick as the assignment sheet landed on his desk. It explained how each group would be expected to create a new product or service from the ground up, and that they had to submit a detailed business plan explaining who their potential customers were (this part had to be backed up by research) and how they would make money (this part required detailed forecasts of start-up costs, as well as a pricing plan). This wasn't even the marketing part yet. Once they had designed the product, they had to create the entire marketing strategy and make the ads. Of course, Lewis expected all materials to be of professional quality.

"Thus," Lewis said, "if, for example, you are an amateur videographer, and you believe that your marketing materials should involve your handsome and hilarious self preening in front of a bedsheet with the name of your product scrawled on it in Magic Marker, you should not expect a passing grade. My former colleagues at Jamison Creative have generously offered training and the use of their facilities during certain preapproved hours, so there is no excuse for producing anything less than professional-quality marketing materials."

Alex had thought he'd be able to spend the next month getting closer to Hanh, but he saw both of their lives sucked into Lewis's project, which he'd somehow forgotten about, despite the fact that Lewis had explained all this when he'd first assigned the individual project. Ugh. Well, at least Dad and Harrison didn't know he'd forgotten all about the most important project of the year.

"Now," Lewis continued, "as teamwork is an essential part of a successful project, you will be working in groups based on the four advisories represented in this class. It is my sincere hope that you have already gotten to know one another, that you understand each other's strengths and weaknesses, and that the relationships you've developed in advisory will help you to form a cohesive team quickly and without rancor."

Alex thought about all the bickering that went on in 212, and it was all he could do not to laugh. He looked around the room and found that he would be working with Savon and Eddie, who would definitely pull their weight and then some, hopefully including his; Tanya, who was a pain in the ass; and Kenisha, who was even more studious than Eddie or Savon. It wasn't a fun feeling to realize that, except maybe for Tanya, he was pretty much the weak link in this group. Then again, Savon, Eddie, and Kenisha probably wouldn't be expecting too much from him, and that might give him some time for Hanh.

Yes, he thought, this could actually work out. Now how long should he wait before he called Hanh?

13

THE FOLLOWING MONDAY, EDDIE wandered from room to room inside FA-CUE looking for Alex. Where was he? They were supposed to have their first group meeting that day after school because they had to present preliminary notes to Lewis in the morning, and Eddie figured he'd probably be the one typing them up. Well, him or Kenisha or Savon, but definitely not Tanya and definitely not Alex, which was why it was such a pain in the butt that he was holding them all up.

He figured he would have to go to Human Resources and ask to use the office phone to call Alex, which would be okay, but, according to Kelvin, could lead to long lectures from whoever was there about how there was a pay phone in the lobby, and how one had to be responsible for making sure one was prepared to make phone calls. Eddie figured he'd probably get a much milder version of any lecture than Kelvin got, but still, he didn't want to listen to a lecture any more than he wanted to troop all the way down to the lobby to try to use a phone that was out of order half the time anyway.

He didn't think Alex would have gone to Melville's now that Sheila was gone, but he didn't seem to be in school, so Eddie figured he should check there. He pushed open the heavy glass door to the lobby and hit the elevator button. After standing there for what seemed like forever, Eddie decided to take the stairs. He flung open the door to the stairwell extra hard, and he heard the unmistakable sound of Alex's voice saying "Ow! Damn!" as the door hit him.

Eddie was just about ready to yell at him—come on, Alex, what the hell are you doing, everybody's waiting for you—but he stopped short when he saw Alex and Hanh untangling themselves from each other's arms as he walked into the stairwell.

They both looked embarrassed, and Alex tried weakly to play it off with "Uh, yeah, so read up to chapter seven I think is the homework."

"Yeah, okay, thanks, Alex," Hanh answered, and ran back into the hallway.

Alex looked sheepish, and though Eddie wanted to yell at him for being late, he figured if he had the chance, he'd rather kiss a girl than go to a meeting, too. Still, he had to give Alex a hard time. "Right, *Hanh* is asking *you* for the homework. That's believable. Can you just imagine if Kelvin had been the one to open the door? Neither one of you would ever hear the end of it."

Alex straightened himself up, regained his composure, and

said, "Yeah, but it wasn't Kelvin. What are you doing here, anyway?"

"I'm looking for the slacker from my group so we can start our marketing meeting!" Eddie said, trying his best to sound annoyed but finding that he was only amused and jealous.

"Oh, crap, is that now?" Alex said, grinning, and Eddie couldn't tell if he was joking or not. "Okay then, let's go," he continued. "We can't stand here all day. You know, it would be a lot easier if Hanh's dad let her out of his sight, but whatever. I mean, if I told Mom and Dad the truth, they'd probably let me go out at night as long as my homework was done, or anyway copied off of yours, but Hanh has a very hard time getting away, you know, so our time together is somewhat limited."

"What are you talking about? You've been on the phone with her for like two hours for the last three nights!"

"Yeah, yeah, on the phone, fine, but that's not the same as the, uh, face-to-face time," and he grinned broadly again.

"Speaking of which, Tanya has to work at six, so we really need to get this meeting done, and you are not going to be popular."

They made their way into 212, where the rest of their group was waiting for them, looking impatient. Kelvin and Gisela's group was meeting in another corner of the room, and all of them, including Hanh, were hard at work, heads bent down over notebooks, which was almost impossible to believe given that the group had Kelvin in it. Eddie supposed Gisela was "keeping him in check," and wondered who was going to keep Alex in check before realizing, sadly, that it was probably him.

Tanya looked up at them and said, "Well, it's about damn time. See, I gotta work in an hour, and I do not have time to be sitting here waiting for your lazy self to get found. You're just lucky that your cousin is in this group, because if I had found you—"

Eddie figured Alex could probably get out of this himself, but he decided to step in anyway, mostly so he could have an excuse to say something to Tanya. "Uh, Tanya, I don't think you're allowed to go where I found him, and I really don't think you would have liked the smell."

Alex played right along, clutching his stomach and saying, "Do *not* get that spicy chicken wrap from downstairs. I'm just saying."

This led to choruses of "Aw, that's nasty" from the rest of the group. Alex and Eddie sat down and got out their notebooks. Eddie lent Alex a pen, and they were ready to begin.

"All right, people," Savon began. "I know y'all have been thinking about phase two of the project ever since phase one, so let's hear your ideas."

"Something with hair," Tanya said. "Like, I don't know, a new dye or relaxer or something."

"You want to research the chemistry behind that stuff?" Alex asked. "Because you know Lewis is going to ask us how our product is chemically different from the other brands on the market, and what makes it better."

"Mmm" was all Tanya said.

The group threw bad ideas around, and Eddie was too nervous to chime in because he was afraid that his idea would sound silly, even though he'd been thinking about it since his first day here. He told himself he should just say it. After all, it couldn't be any worse than Alex's suggestion—a directory rating which coffee shops had the cutest baristas—an idea he'd probably thought of between the stairwell and 212.

Finally Tanya looked at him—Tanya! Looked at him! Usually he just looked at her while drooling, as Savon had noticed. She said, "Okay, Left Eye, what do you got? Because nobody else has anything good, and I am not doing any of these stupid ideas, especially Alex's, which he obviously thought up while he was sitting on the toilet for two minutes."

"Well, um, promise not to laugh, okay."

Everybody rolled their eyes and Tanya said, "Not only will I not laugh, I will personally kiss you if you can get me out of this meeting so I can go do something that actually makes me some money."

Eddie hoped that his ears weren't turning red, though he knew they were, and decided he had to start talking before his mind tied itself in knots. He knew she was joking about the kiss, but still, a girl wouldn't say that to a guy she wouldn't really consider kissing. Would she?

"Um, well, okay, you guys remember how Kelvin was late to advisory the other day?"

At this Kelvin called out from the other side of the room, "Who's saying my name? You got beef, Left Eye? Ow!" The last part came as Gisela dope-slapped him on the back of his head and told him to get back to work.

"Well, every morning at home they listen to the radio and there are always these traffic reports, you know, 'Tobin Bridge is backed up to the tolls,' 'Expressway heavy and slow from the split,' this kind of thing, and I thought maybe it would be great to have some kind of traffic report that kids who live in the city could use, like, so you'd know before you left the house if somebody in Codfish Square—" There were snickers at this, and Savon chimed in with "Codman, Left Eye." Eddie continued, "Right. Anyway, if there was a problem there or something, you'd have the information and you could take another bus or whatever."

No one said anything, and Eddie felt like he had to fill the silence. "So, yeah, probably it's a dumb idea."

"I don't think it's dumb," Kenisha said.

"Me neither," Tanya said. "Shoot, I'd love to know to stay out of Forest Hills when my ex-boyfriend's fool crew is there looking to start something." Ex-boyfriend?

"Yeah," Savon added.

They debated how this service would be delivered, without reaching any conclusions. Still, they all agreed that they had enough for Eddie to type up something respectable for the preliminary notes. They gathered up their stuff to go, and Tanya was already at the door by the time everybody else had their notebooks in their bags.

Alex yelled out, "Hey, Tanya, don't you owe my boy here a kiss? He ended the meeting!"

"Yeah, some other time," she said, and was gone. Eddie knew it was never going to happen, but he was still disappointed, because he did kind of wish he could at least get to feel Tanya's lips on his cheek. On the other hand, he couldn't wait till he and Alex were alone so he could punch him, or at least remind him that, as the only other person who knew

about him and Hanh, he had the power to make Alex's life
hell.

That night, Eddie sat at the computer trying to organize
everybody's ideas that he had scribbled in his notebook. He
had expected this, and it was good for two reasons. One was
that he preferred doing it himself to having his grade riding
on something Alex might produce, and the other was that if
he was really busy with schoolwork, that took up a huge slice
of the pie chart of his mind, and Tanya, with her thing about
kissing him, was taking up another big slice of his mind,
which shrank the Mom slice down to a quite manageable size.

But then Alex started bugging him.

"So, uh, Eddie, what do you say to a little excursion?"

"Alex, I have to type our proposal, and it's already eight."

"Yeah, I know, but Hanh gets a break at nine and she wants
me to meet her for bubble tea."

"So go meet her! I'm trying to get this done so we can get a
good grade!"

"Aw, I don't think Mom and Dad would really go for that.
You know, Dad's been talking to Harrison, and my homework's not exactly done, and there is no way they're gonna let
me go out and have fun until all my homework is done, and
I've got at least another hour here. But then I thought, you
know, if you were like a little upset, we could go for a walk or
something . . ."

"Alex . . ." Eddie found himself too angry to speak. This was
his life, his real life, and Alex wanted him to use it as a cover

story just so Alex could get out of finishing his homework and meet up with a girl while Eddie sat there feeling like an idiot! Plus, he had been pleasantly thinking about school and Tanya, and Alex had ruined everything by reminding him of Mom. In his imagination, he wheeled around and punched Alex in the nose in one smooth motion, and Alex, blood running down his face, said, "Oh, man, I'm sorry, I'm a total asshole."

But in reality all he could manage to do was grit his teeth and say, "You are a really selfish kid."

Alex stood there with his mouth hanging open like an idiot, like it had never occurred to him that he was selfish. Eddie started typing again, even though the screen was a little blurry at first. Finally, Alex walked out without saying anything else.

Eddie did get the proposal done, and, checking to make sure Alex wasn't back or lurking outside the door, he took Mom's letter out from under the bed and read it again. He didn't really want to, but he was already thinking about her, thanks to Alex. It had been a few days, and he knew he should write back because that's what the good guys do, right? They say, "All is forgiven, Mom. I love you, too. Get better and come back."

But he couldn't do that. He wasn't sure he wanted to see his mom again. And he didn't know if he could forgive her. He did hope she would get better, but he was pretty sure he never ever wanted to go back to Oldham. He really liked this new life. Most of the time he could kind of forget that it had actually been him who lived in Oldham, he could just look at it like it was somebody else's life, somebody dead. But Mom kept popping up like some zombie from the past, still out there, staggering down the street and going, "Edddddiiee . . . I'm coming baaaaaaaack . . ."

He laughed at that idea, mostly to stop himself from crying.

And he got out a piece of paper and tried for the third time to write his mom back.

Dear Mom,
  How are you?

Stupid. He ripped out the paper and tore it up. Then he tried again.

Dear Mom,
  I got your letter.

Weak. He crumpled this one and threw it in the direction of the trash can. He knew he had to write what he really wanted to say. And then maybe he'd produce a clean version to actually send to her later. But he couldn't write something nice to her before he wrote what he really felt.

Dear Mom,
  I'm glad you're getting better. It's good that you are sorry for the bad stuff you did, but I don't want to hear about it all, and I damn sure don't want to read ten pages where you talk about every stupid thing you did that I am trying my best to forget because you need to apologize. See, you're still really only thinking of yourself. Selfish, just like Alex. Maybe I don't need to hear

about it right now! Did that ever occur to you or any of the ge-niuses at the Hotel Rehab? I guess not. I wish I could say I for-give you and it's okay and I'm not mad, but I'm still really really mad at you for not being a regular mom. I know you said think-ing about me is what's getting you better, but, I mean, isn't it kind of late for that? You never thought about me before you needed me to get you better! So Eddie has to take care of everything again! Because Eddie is so mature for his age! I hate you, Mom. Never write me again.

At this point Eddie was crying so hard he couldn't see the paper, and his tears were splattering the ink anyway, so he threw his notebook down on the floor and curled up on his bed and cried and cried because he felt completely alone.

14

SELFISH? ALEX SAT AT THE TABLE pretending to do his homework and wondering if he really was selfish. Just because he wanted to get a little help from his cousin to leave the house?

He'd been making a huge effort—hell, it wasn't even an effort anymore—he just included Eddie in everything, laughed at teachers with him, scoped out girls with him, and had his back whenever Savon or Kelvin tried to dis him.

But, then again, it was kind of cheesy to try and get Eddie to pretend to be upset about his mom. Alex heard him crying late at night often enough to know that he didn't need to pretend to be upset, and maybe that part was kind of selfish.

Still, he'd only wanted to get out and see his girlfriend! Was that so wrong? Probably not, but as he thought about it, he figured that the way he did it might have been wrong. He could have pretended to be doing laundry and gone down in the elevator, but left the house instead of going to the basement. And Eddie probably would have covered for him. Dumb. Why didn't he think of that before? He guessed that girls made him do dumb stuff. Although it wasn't like he'd never done any dumb stuff before he got interested in girls. Damn—with Mom and Dad on his back all the time at home, and Harrison and Lewis and pretty much every other adult on his back at school, he'd just managed to piss off his best ally and, this was a weird thought, probably his best friend.

He went back to their bedroom door to try to say he was sorry, but he could hear Eddie crying in there, and he didn't want to go in while that was going on. So he went to the couch and turned on the TV. He should do something nice for Eddie, something purely unselfish. Eddie never said anything, but he was obviously totally into Tanya, which seemed like an odd choice to Alex, but there had probably been stranger couples in the history of the world. So maybe he could help out a little bit.

The next morning, Eddie was acting normal again, and as they ate their organic cinnamon puffs, Alex said, "Uh, Eddie, I'm sorry about last night. That was kind of a dumb thing for me to ask you."

Eddie looked at him for a minute, then said, "Yeah, well, it's okay. I guess if I had T—a girl waiting for me, I'd probably do the same thing."

"Yeah, you'd sell me out in a heartbeat for a piece of tail. That's what all the ladies say, anyway."

Eddie punched him, smiling, and said, "Yeah, that's why all the ladies steer clear of me. They're afraid of getting their hearts broken."

"Sure, dawg, you got a bad rep, you know, mackin' all over Oldham, had to skip town 'cause of the baby mama drama." Alex laughed, imagining Eddie tooling around the suburbs in a pimpmobile with little sons and daughters. Eddie laughed, too, so everything was cool between them.

Unfortunately, it wasn't as cool with Hanh because she had waited for him at the bubble tea place and he had been so busy thinking about how he wasn't selfish that he hadn't called her back. She gave him dirty looks all day, and he tried and failed to catch her alone. He called her at lunch, but she wouldn't answer her phone. He basically didn't know what to do. He was really glad that girls were not exactly like boys in most ways, but he did kind of wish that when they were mad at you, you could just make a joke and they would punch you and everything would be okay.

The next day, Hanh ignored him all day. After school, they had to go meet with Lewis as a group to get their proposal notes back. Alex was annoyed. Why couldn't Lewis have these meetings during class instead of giving those boring lectures? Alex was also nervous. Not because he was worried about the grade, but because he really needed to go down to Hanh's place and try to patch things up, and if this meeting took too long, he was going to be late for dinner, and then he'd be in trouble with his parents, which would be worth it if he was back on Hanh's good side but would be a serious bummer if he wasn't.

Alex was the last member of his group to arrive at the marketing room. And all he'd done was go to the bathroom, run downstairs to get a drink, and look around the lobby for Hanh for a few minutes. Jeez.

"Ah, Mr. Scoville. I'm delighted you are able to make the meeting. And I'm sorry to inform everyone else that they've lost five points on this part of the assignment due to your unprofessional tardiness!"

The other members of the group began to grumble, but Lewis cut them off with "Let us remember that we never air our differences in front of the client, and let us remember that the client in this case is me. Whatever tension exists outside of this setting, in here you display unity. Should you wish to beat Mr. Scoville senseless once I've left, that is of course your business, though I would suggest that you don't do that on school property or leave any visible marks, as a black eye might hinder Mr. Scoville's attempts to present himself professionally." Lewis gave a little smile, and Alex clamped his teeth together and looked at his desk. Why was this guy being such a jerk about him being a little late? Now everybody was going to be even madder at him.

"Fortunately for all of you and perhaps especially for Mr. Scoville, the five-point deduction leaves your grade at a 90, which is an A minus and still the highest grade of any group in this class. You have simply thought outside the box in a way no other group has, and I commend you. Now, that having been said, there are still many unanswered questions about your proposal. Do take note, because I'm giving you these questions only in oral form."

Alex watched as Kenisha, Savon, Eddie, and even Tanya got out pens and notebooks. Alex rummaged through his bag for a notebook and whispered, "Eddie! Pen?" while Lewis gave him a disapproving look. Stupid. Not like all five of them had to take notes anyway, but whatever.

"First, how will you collect your data? Second, how will your customers access the traffic reports? Third, and most important, what's your model for making money? Will your customers pay for this information? Will radio stations pay for it? Will it be advertiser-sponsored? Obviously you won't have time to have done thorough research or run the numbers, but I'll expect preliminary answers to these questions tomorrow." He paused here as everybody gasped. "One of my tasks here is to get you accustomed to working under pressure. I think you'll find me a demanding client, but it's my hope that this experience will allow you to keep your cool when dealing with demanding clients in the private sector. That will be all, and good day."

The group packed up their notebooks and filed into the hall. Alex was at the door when Lewis said, "Mr. Scoville, a moment please." Alex looked at his watch and felt like jumping out of his skin. He had to get down to Chinatown! And he didn't have time to listen to some boring lecture.

"Alex," Lewis said, and his voice sounded different—not all stiff and formal—and this was the first time Lewis had ever used his first name. "You've got the role of the charming, funny screw-up down pretty well." This was so unfair! Charming, okay, but Kelvin was the funny screw-up! "I don't think you should settle for that. You're capable of a lot more. I can tell you from my decades of experience in the private sector that your intelligence and charisma can take you very far. However, so far you've been riding the charisma and totally neglecting the intelligence. Why is that?"

"Uh, I don't know." Jerk. What did he mean about Alex neglecting his intelligence? He used his intelligence all the time, like for coming up with excuses. Though actually Eddie was even better at that than Alex was.

"You can continue to coast by on what's easy for you and remain at C level pretty much forever. Or you can actually put some effort into something, and there will be no limit to the doors that will open for you."

"Uh, okay."

"Okay, then. See you tomorrow."

"Yeah," Alex said, walking out the door. This was why he hated this place, hated Lewis, hated all adults. They all thought they had you all figured out. Oh, yeah, I see you for an hour every day, so I know all about you, I can tell you about yourself. Jerk. And that crap about closing doors again. It was like they all had the same corny script, and they read from different parts.

Alex really wanted to stalk off and be mad for a while, but the rest of the group was waiting in the hall.

Savon—Savon, of all people—punched him quickly and hard on the upper arm five times. "That's one for every point we lost. You're lucky I didn't let Tanya at you."

"I have never gotten an A at this damn school," Tanya said. "If I don't get one because of you, I'm gonna slap you so hard your whole family will feel it."

Alex couldn't help smiling. "See, it's your soft feminine side that's so charming. At least that's what your boyfriend shaking the cup full of change outside said."

"Kids, kids," Savon said, "where's the love in this group? We gotta work together, y'all."

"Yeah," Kenisha said. "I can only imagine how many points we'll lose if you actually do slap him."

"Yeah," Eddie said, "Mr. Lewis would be like, 'I note that Mr. Scoville has a terribly unprofessional red handprint upon his cheek. Fifteen-point deduction.' " Kenisha and Savon laughed, and even Tanya smiled a little.

"Okay, okay," Savon said, "listen. We are going to have to meet in advisory at 8 a.m. to answer these questions. Everybody better be thinking about this all night long, and have some dreams about it, and don't be coming in at 8:10 talking about 'Oh, I forgot.' " Savon looked at Alex.

"I got my one free period of the week tomorrow, so I'll type stuff up if y'all come in with some ideas that ain't stupid," Savon said, looking at Eddie.

"Dag, who put you in charge?" Alex asked.

"Uh," Eddie piped up, "actually we did in the first meeting while you were, uh, in the *bathroom*." He said that funny, like he wanted people to know Alex wasn't really in the bathroom. Everybody was just piling on Alex today. Fine.

"Left Eye," Savon said, "you better get your cousin here on time."

"Yes sir, Soap sir!" Eddie said, and saluted, and everybody went their separate ways.

Alex grabbed Eddie's sleeve. "Listen, man, I gotta go down

to Hanh's place, she's all mad at me, and I can't let it go another day and I really can't wait until all my homework's done. Will you cover with Mom and Dad?"

"I . . . uh . . . I've got my appointment . . ." Alex could see Eddie getting annoyed, and he hoped there wasn't another lecture coming, because he didn't think he could deal with that today. Fortunately, all Eddie said was "Okay. I'll tell them that you and Savon had to stay behind to work on project stuff."

Eddie was awesome. Alex figured that tomorrow he could put Operation Tanya into action for him. For now, Alex left school and took the train downtown, making a couple of stops before arriving outside of Pho Saigon. He thought about walking in, but then he figured if he got Hanh in trouble with her dad, it wouldn't help his cause. He went around back, into the alley that Pho Saigon shared with three other restaurants, a jewelry store, and a market. There were five stinking Dumpsters back here, and Alex started wondering if this was a dumb idea. He stood at the back door, trying to ignore the garbage smell. He called her, but of course she didn't answer, so he sent a text message: IM AT YR BACK DR. PLS OPEN UP.

He watched as his phone told him, "Message sent successfully!" and waited and waited, watching the minutes tick by on his phone. After five minutes, he was getting mad, and he was about to leave when the door creaked open. He hoped it wasn't Hanh's dad about to chuck a bag of garbage toward the Dumpster, because if it was, he'd probably hit Alex in the face with it.

Fortunately, it was Hanh. "What?" she asked in an annoyed voice, and Alex found that the speech he'd been rehearsing just sort of evaporated out of his head once he saw her face. He handed her a bubble tea, a single rose, and a shiny balloon that said SORRY on it.

Hanh took the stuff and tried to keep scowling, but she couldn't help smiling. "Now, see, where am I going to put all this stuff?" she said. "You're just lucky you're cute," she told Alex, and she kissed him. "Now get out of here. And call me tonight."

Sometime later, Alex found himself outside his house, thinking that he must have floated there.

15

AT THERAPY, DON HAD TOLD EDDIE
it was good he'd expressed his anger in an unsendable letter to
his mom. However, the sooner he wrote and mailed an actual
letter to her the better because "you're carrying it around un-
written, in your head, and it's obviously weighing you down,
which you don't need in the middle of a big school project."

So now he was sitting in the middle of a pile of crumpled-up
paper. He crumpled up another one, kind of imagining it was
Mom's face while he did it. He got out another piece of paper
and started to write. He'd gotten as far as *Dear Mom, You selfish
bitch* when Alex burst through the door.

"Oh yeah!" he said. "Yeah, I am Mr. Smooth, and she forgave me, and she gave me a big kiss, and I have you to thank
for the smooth cover-up at home, you are the man, Edward,
you . . . oh. Hey, what's wrong?"

Eddie figured there was no way to disguise it, because he was really upset and sitting in a pile of unfinished letters, and anyway Alex now owed him at least two, and he was tired of carrying this whole thing around by himself, so he said, "Well, you know, I got that letter from my mom, and I figure I should write her back. But . . . but . . . I don't . . . I feel like I should tell her 'It's all okay, I forgive you,' but I don't forgive her, I hate her! I hate her! What kind of way is that to feel about your mom? This sucks! I hate her and I hate hating her, and I hate . . . I can't even think about anything else until I get this letter written. I tried to work on the project . . ."

He looked at Alex. He felt completely crushed by his life right now, and he wished he could just take it easy all the time like Alex did, but Alex had it easy, and he never would . . .

"Okay," Alex said, and Eddie was really glad he hadn't tried to hug him or something. "Well, why do you have to write her back?"

"Because she's in rehab, she's waiting for my letter because I'm a beacon in her darkness or some damn thing, and if she screws this up, there is no way I'm going to be walking around feeling like it's my fault."

"So what do you have so far?"

" 'I hate you, you selfish bitch,' stuff like that. I obviously can't send her anything like that, but I can't say, 'Thanks for the letter, Mom, it's all okay,' either."

"See, now this is where you need my expertise. You're trying to do something hard, right, and you want to get out of it, and who is the champion in that department?"

"What, do you have a letter already written? Do I get to

copy off you for a change?" The idea actually made Eddie smile for the first time in hours. He was glad Alex was here.

"Hilarious. No. Your first mistake is trying to write a letter. Let's think postcard. Here, I always grab these at restaurants, especially if there's a hot girl on them." He rooted around in his desk drawer and handed Eddie a postcard. "Okay, so what does she need to hear that you can stand to say?"

"Um, I don't know. I guess, 'I got your letter, I'm glad you're getting better, I still love you,' or something."

"Great! Start that off with a 'Dear Mom,' and you're golden!"

Eddie considered this. He couldn't really send his mom a three-sentence postcard. Could he? Then again, he also couldn't spend the next three weeks not writing a two-page letter. Well, what the hell. It was better than nothing, and then it would be done. He wrote "Dear Mom" and followed it with the three sentences he'd said earlier and signed it "Love, Eddie." He dug into his notebook, found the address of the treatment center, addressed the postcard, and held it up to read again.

Suddenly Alex was laughing. Eddie started to get mad, but then Alex said, "Uh, dude, oh, I'm sorry, but I . . . I just think you'd better send a different postcard."

Eddie turned over the postcard. There was a beautiful, sweaty woman with colossal boobs and her red-fingernailed hands wrapped around the neck of a bottle, and at the bottom of the card it said "Frost Vodka Makes Me Hot!" Eddie started to laugh, too. "Yeah, I guess . . ." he couldn't finish his sentence because he was laughing too hard.

"Not the greatest thing to send the booze ad to the rehab facility," Alex continued, and Eddie kept laughing, because the whole thing was just so stupid, and it really wasn't funny at all, but that didn't stop him.

Eventually they collected themselves, and Alex gave him a postcard with a picture of what Eddie would have sworn was the same sweaty woman from the vodka postcard, but this one was a cologne ad, so Eddie figured that was okay. When he went to bed that night, he chuckled thinking about a vodka postcard showing up at the rehab clinic, and right before he fell asleep, he realized that this was the first night he'd gone to bed feeling happy in a really long time.

The next day, Eddie was nervous walking into advisory. He had tried to think about the project last night, but then he got involved in writing his postcard, and then he was tired, and now he was walking into a meeting with nothing at all prepared. He hated the sick feeling in his stomach. He really couldn't understand how Alex did this all the time.

Kelvin and Aisha and Gisela were doing homework, and Savon and Tanya were sitting there waiting for them. "Damn!" Tanya said. "I can't believe Alex is here before Kenisha! Nice work, Left Eye!"

"Yeah," Savon added, "this is the first time that boy's been on time for anything. You better just make sure you grab him right at the end of school so he doesn't cost us more points."

At this, Kelvin piped in. "Oh, shoot, losing points! See now, I hate to start this in the advisory, because we're like family and all, but it looks like the smart side of the family is sitting over here! We ain't had no extra meetings with Lewis. Y'all's proposal must be horrible, yo!" Kelvin was grinning really broadly. "It's gonna be tough workin' for me when y'all get older, but don't worry, I'll be fair."

"Gee," Alex said, "I didn't know panhandlers got a staff! You gonna have some begging-for-change trainees? Talkin' 'bout 'Shake the cup like this, sonny!' "

Before Kelvin could reply, Tanya busted out with "So what did you get on your proposal?"

"Eighty-three!" Kelvin said. He stood up, puffed out his chest, and said, "What? What?" staring at Tanya.

"I don't know why y'all are over there talking about 'What, what' when the only reason we got an 83 is because I did all the work," Gisela said.

"Aw, you know that's a lie," Kelvin said.

"Well, we got a 90!" Tanya said. She stood and said, "What? What? Oh, you ain't got so much to say now, do you, Kelvin? Yeah, better know the facts before you open your mouth next time!"

At that moment, Kenisha walked in with her head down. "Sorry, everybody," she said. "It won't happen again, I promise."

"That's okay," Alex said, "but Savon gets to punch you five times."

"Shut up, Alex," Savon said. "All right, let's get this meeting started, and somebody please tell me you got something for me. Left Eye, you start."

Oh no. They were all looking at him, looking for him to save the day. And he was just no good at thinking of stuff on the fly like Alex could. This was not going to be pretty.

"Well, uh . . ." he began.

"I'm sorry, Eddie, is it okay if I go first? I think I have some good stuff," Kenisha said.

"Uh, well, sure, I guess," Eddie said.

"I called my cousin who works at Hot 95, and he said there is no way their advertisers would ever go for this kind of thing, because it's mostly suburban white kids—sorry, guys"— she smiled at Eddie and Alex—"but anyway, suburban white kids who listen to the station, and the station's afraid they'll lose their richest listeners if they seem too ghetto.

"So I got off the phone with my cousin, and I tried to call Hanh, but she didn't answer, so I had to log on to my e-mail to send her a text message, since my grandmom won't let me have a cell phone, and there was this ad next to my in box where you can sign up to get sports scores and stuff messaged to your phone. So I thought that we could—that people could sign up to get the information messaged to their phones, and then there could be an ad with the traffic report, you know, like 'Eat at Costa Pizza' or something."

The group was silent. Finally Savon spoke. "That's some good stuff. I'm throwing my idea away right now."

"Way, way better than what I had," Eddie said, drawing an approving look from Alex.

At the end of the day, Eddie headed to the stairwell and waited there until Alex walked in. "Hi, honey!" he said to

Alex. "No time to make out today, big meeting with Mr. Lewis!"

"Aw, come on, Eddie, man, five minutes. What's it gonna hurt?"

"Dude, it's going to hurt you if we lose more points and I let Tanya get after you."

"Yeah, you'd like to get Tanya after you."

Eddie blushed and pulled Alex by the arm into the hallway. "Shut up about that."

"Ooo, touchy!"

They saw Hanh in the hall, and Eddie said, "Meeting. Lewis. Can't be late." He looked over at Alex, who was pointing at him with this "Can you believe this guy?" expression on his face.

They arrived outside of Lewis's room at the same time as the rest of the group. Tanya looked at them and smiled approvingly. "Okay then, Left Eye. That's what I'm talkin' about. Damn, I'm glad you are on this team, or we'd be waiting for his sorry ass all afternoon."

Eddie could feel himself blushing, and he wished he had some clever comeback, but all he could come up with was "Uh, well, uh, okay, um, I guess everybody's here, so, uh, let's go in." Mr. Smooth. Whatever smoothness Alex had did not seem to run in the family, or at least not over to Eddie's side.

Lewis practically gushed over their plan. He said "push marketing" so many times that it started to sound kind of dirty, and Eddie thought he would crack up if Lewis said it one more time or if he looked at Alex, who he could tell was holding back a laugh himself. So he kept his head down and took notes. After what seemed like forever, Lewis said, "Very impressive. I am genuinely looking forward to the next phase. That will be all, and good day."

Afterward, the group convened in the hallway. "Okay," Savon said. "The way I'm thinking, we need a Web site designed where people can sign up for the service, we gotta get some advertisers to pay the bills, and we need some ads of our own to attract customers to the site. Oh yeah, we also need traffic reporters. I think it makes more sense for us to split up and work on different tasks instead of us all trying to do everything at once. I can probably do the Web design and research how we send these messages out from a server."

"Great!" Alex piped up. "Kenisha and I will hit some businesses asking whether they'd be interested in this and how much they'd pay for it. Eddie and Tanya can work on the marketing." He shot Eddie a look. Eddie believed it meant something like "You can thank me later." He hoped he wasn't turning red again, but his face and ears were starting to feel hot.

"Why are you dividing it up that way? You know you need Left Eye to make you do any work!" Tanya said.

"Because Kenisha explains this really well, much better than anybody else, because it's her idea. And because I have the charm that every good salesman needs."

Tanya said, "Oh yeah, 'I'm late 'cause I couldn't get out of the bathroom.' Real smooth."

"Shut up, Tanya. What, are you gonna be like, 'Oh, I'd love to explain this to y'all, but you know I do have to go braid some hair, so bump you.' "

"Okay, okay, remember the love, and save the attitude for Kelvin," Savon said, and everybody but Tanya smiled.

"Okay, well, at least if I'm with Left Eye, I know some work is gonna get done," Tanya said, and Eddie saw Alex get that glint in his eye like he was going to make some joke about getting to work, or working it out, or something like that, but thankfully he didn't.

Eddie and Alex didn't say anything until they were on the bus. Then Alex busted out with "So you gonna thank me, or what?"

Eddie didn't know what to say, so he punched Alex on the arm.

"Okay, I see how it is. This is the thanks I get. You know they would have put us together so you could babysit me, but I worked out the preemptive strike. So now you get to work on some puuuuuuuuuush marketing"—he drew that phrase out and made it sound way dirtier than it already did—"with Tanya instead of looking at me every day after school, but that's fine, go ahead and punch me, I don't mind, I just do good deeds for the sake of doing them."

Eddie laughed. And then he started to imagine actually spending time working alone with Tanya, and he started to feel terrified. He'd never really talked to Alex about Tanya before, but he'd kept the secret about Hanh for so long, and he knew so much about Alex from living with him, that Alex wouldn't dare spill his business. "I don't know, do you think Tanya, I mean, do you think she . . . could I . . ." he trailed off because he was so embarrassed that it actually hurt.

"Well, I don't know. I mean, honestly, I've never known her

to go out with a white guy before . . . I mean there was that one guy who looked kinda white, but I guess he was Dominican or something. But then again, she has never felt the pull of that Eddie magnetism before. Maybe you could be the first. Anyway, you know you won't have a chance if all you do is stare at her in advisory."

Eddie took a minute to chew on this. It didn't sound good. Tanya was hot, and he wasn't, but she did seem to appreciate that he was helping the group. Eddie had no idea if this was the kind of thing that impressed girls, since he hadn't really had any experience talking to or trying to impress girls before this year. He knew at OHS that "Hey baby, I got a hell of a good grade on my project" would have gotten you laughed at by pretty much any girl. But it was okay to get good grades at FA-CUE, so maybe the girls here actually would be impressed by an A.

And what about her not dating white guys? Eddie didn't really know what to think about that. He believed in his mind that anybody could date anybody. He never thought it was weird for a minute that Alex was going out with Hanh, or sneaking around with Hanh, or whatever you called it, but now when he found that the white girl he liked might not date white guys, he felt weird. Would he feel weird if he heard that a black girl didn't date white guys? He didn't think so.

He wondered if learning to talk a little more black like Alex and Tanya did would help his case with Tanya. Or did he even have a case? He didn't know.

He probably wouldn't know until he and Tanya got together for training at Jamison Creative so they could create some marketing materials. He had a hard time falling asleep that night, because he was trying to imagine how exactly he would approach Tanya about this. He knew it was pretty simple, really—just go up to her and say something like "So when do you want to do this?" but he couldn't figure out exactly how he was supposed to do that without stumbling over his words and acting stupid and having everybody knowing he liked her. Although if Savon and Alex knew already, maybe everybody else knew. Which would be bad.

As Eddie drifted off, he realized again that even if this stuff about Tanya was a stupid dream, it was a lot more fun than worrying about his mom.

16

THE NEXT MORNING, ALEX WAS still feeling buzzed from his success at implementing phase one of Operation Tanya. Nobody could say that he had done anything selfish, and doing something good for somebody else actually made him feel kind of good, too. Of course, getting Eddie closer to Tanya might just mean that he was closer to getting his feelings hurt. Well, you can't win if you don't play, like they always said on those lottery commercials. Alex wasn't going to drive himself nuts thinking. That was Eddie's job.

Although now that he was doing some thinking, he had to admit he was a little worried about how stuff was going with Hanh. She had been nice and forgiven him and even met him after school at Melville's, where they held hands like a real couple and drank their lattes, and it was corny as hell, but

Alex didn't care. It was fun and exciting, too. He just wondered how they were going to find time for each other with all this project stuff. Already she had gotten pissed when he accidentally blew her off and stayed home, and he figured she would probably be twice as pissed when she found out he had to spend a whole bunch of days running around town with Kenisha. Though if she looked in the mirror, she'd realize she had nothing to be jealous about, but Alex knew that girls' minds didn't work that way. Or at least Hanh's didn't.

While they were waiting for the bus, Eddie stammered, "Um, so, uh, let me ask you something," and started blushing immediately, so Alex knew it was about Tanya.

"Shoot," Alex said.

"I have to ask her, you know, just about working together, and stuff—"

"I'm sorry, who are we talking about?" Alex grinned. He knew he was being obnoxious, but he just couldn't help it.

"Ha ha. Anyway, so I don't know how to—I mean, I don't want to make her think I like her or something . . ."

"Even though you do." When Alex said this, Eddie looked around like he thought somebody from school might be at the bus stop, though there was nobody there except some yuppie lady in a suit and her boyfriend, who was all shabby-looking.

"Yeah. Okay, yeah. So I just . . . I'm afraid . . . I'm going to sound goofy and stupid like I'm doing now, only with Kelvin pointing and laughing."

"I think maybe you need a calendar or something. Just have

some times and dates ready and then you can stare at the calendar the whole time and try not to look down her shirt or
think about how incredibly hot she is."

"Jesus, Alex, I wasn't even thinking about looking down her
shirt!" Eddie said, then turned around. Alex noticed the yuppie and her hippie boyfriend smiling.

The bus came, and they rode in silence to the Francis Abernathy Center for Urban Education. As they were getting off
the bus, the yuppie lady, who was sitting sideways near the
front of the bus, said to Eddie, "Just tell her, kid. Life's too
short." Her scraggly boyfriend shook his head no and made
these hand signals that said, "Don't listen to her. She doesn't
know what she's talking about," and then stopped when she
looked over at him.

Alex figured that just about summed it up. As much as he
pretended to be Mr. Smooth because he had his fifth girlfriend in two years, he didn't really know what Eddie should
do. Nobody knew anything when it came to this stuff.

They got into 212, and Kelvin was arguing with Gisela and
Aisha, apparently about whether women could rap.

Alex sat and took out his history notes and thought he
might study for today's quiz, mostly because this argument
was boring. Tanya was actually studying, and Alex watched approvingly as Eddie made sure to approach her while Kelvin
was busy yelling at Gisela and Aisha.

Alex still had his notebook open and pretended to study
while eavesdropping on Eddie and Tanya.

"Okay," Eddie said, staring at his little assignment book, "so
I guess we need . . . um, we have to . . ." Oh no! He was going

down in flames! Alex wanted to rescue him, but he knew Eddie had to sink or swim on his own here.

Fortunately for Eddie, Tanya herself came to his rescue. "Okay, we gotta make an appointment at Jamison, so can you do that today because I have to be at the shop right after school. Just tell me when it is and I'll get off work. Obviously we gotta meet before we go in there to figure out what we're doing, but I'm mad busy and I can't stay after, so here's my cell phone number, call me after eight tonight and we'll work it out."

Unfortunately for Eddie, there had been a silent break in the argument as Tanya said the last part, which meant that Kelvin had heard.

"All right, then, Left Eye!" Kelvin said. "My boy! Got the digits! That's what I'm talking about! And Tanya was all, call me and we'll *work it out.* Yeah, Left Eye! Who's the mack?"

Alex looked over at Eddie, who looked very much like he wanted to crawl under a table and die as Tanya said, "We're talking about project stuff, dummy! See, that's why I hate this advisory, because y'all are mad ignorant and always got something to say even when you don't know nothing. Always gotta open your mouth, talkin' trash."

"Okay, Tanya, you want to play it off, I understand, you know, don't want the whole advisory up in your business, I understand, embarrassed about your little thing with Left Eye, I understand that, too," Kelvin said, and Alex felt like he had to jump in.

Amazingly, though, Eddie beat him to it. He actually had a smile on his face instead of looking embarrassed or mad.

"Yeah, Kelvin, and *you're* just embarrassed about your little *thing*."

"Oh!" Gisela roared, clapping Eddie on the back as everybody laughed. Savon called out, "Check please!" Kelvin, for once in his life, had absolutely nothing to say.

Stuff was pretty quiet after that. Kenisha came in and gave Alex a list of businesses they were meeting with, along with contact names and a paragraph summary of what each place's business was and how they currently marketed to urban teens. So all Alex had to do was basically show up and BS these guys into saying they thought the idea was great. He loved working with Kenisha.

Harrison arrived with the usual boring announcements, and Hanh came in late. Alex tried to catch her eye, but she wouldn't even look at him. What the hell was that about? They had coffee yesterday! There was no possible way he'd done anything wrong between then and now. Was there? He tried to remember if there was something that he hadn't done, but he couldn't think of anything. Did he say something to piss her off yesterday? He didn't think so. They just sort of talked about what happened in school and then sat there holding hands and not saying anything. Was he in trouble for that? He was used to getting in trouble for things he said at school and at home, but this looked like it might be the first time he'd ever gotten in trouble for something he didn't say. Well, whatever. He wasn't buying any flowers for this one. He decided not to worry about it.

Except he sort of did. He didn't see her after school, so he called her while he and Kenisha were waiting (and waiting and waiting in the cold) for the 22 bus. He figured that if Kenisha and Hanh were calling and messaging each other, she probably knew what was going on. In any case, Kenisha was not the kind of person to go running to tell Kelvin stuff.

Hanh picked up on the fourth ring. "Hey," she said in a kind of flat way.

"Hey!" Alex tried to bring enough enthusiasm to the conversation for both of them. "What's up?"

"Nothing. Just trying to get my homework done. I'm supposed to meet with some fools from the 216 advisory to study for a math test, and I'm not looking forward to it."

"Mmm. Who is it?"

"It's really just one person I don't get along with, but it's a long story, and I gotta go."

Well, that was quick. "Uh, okay, sure. I'm just . . . uh . . . are you okay?"

Sounding tired, annoyed, and like she was lying, Hanh said, "Yeah, I'm fine, everything's fine, I'll talk to you tomorrow, okay?"

Before Alex could say anything, Hanh had hung up. Alex took a minute to just look at his phone and feel puzzled.

"Mmm-hmmm," Kenisha said, smiling.

"What? What do you know?"

"Come on now, Alex, I would never betray the confidence of a friend. You know Hanh's my girl. I can't go around telling people what she tells me."

"Come on, Kenisha. We're partners here! We gotta work together! And anyway, 212 is like family, you can't have secrets in a family!"

"So you want me to tell Kelvin and the rest of the family about you and Hanh?"

"Uh, well, not really, I guess. But if you . . ."

"I'm just playing. I haven't talked to Hanh in two days. She's mad busy all the time. I just wanted to mess with you." She paused for a minute. "That was mean. I'm sorry."

"Nah, don't worry about it. You know if you liked one of my friends, I'd be messing with your mind every day."

Kenisha's face changed instantly, and she looked at him kind of funny. "She didn't say . . ." she began, and then stopped talking and looked at the ground.

"She didn't say what?"

"Nothing." Now she was digging in her bag and wouldn't look at Alex. What was that about? Well, she obviously wasn't going to tell him.

So that was that, but as they rode the 22 to Blue Hill Avenue, Alex wondered if Kenisha really did know something. Something was definitely going on. Alex figured he'd find out tomorrow, and once again he decided not to worry.

This time he came closer to succeeding because he spent the next two hours being a charming screw-up, or whatever Lewis had called him, who screwed up so much he got eight businesses on Blue Hill Avenue to agree to advertise on the teen traffic report that didn't even exist. Three guys tried to cut him checks right there in the store, they loved the idea so much. Take that, Lewis. Take that, Harrison. Take that, Mom and Dad. Looks like I just opened a whole bunch of doors, Alex thought.

17

EDDIE GOT HOME WELL BEFORE
Alex. He had to call Tanya after eight. He had made the appointment at Jamison Creative but he realized he didn't have any idea what they were going to create.

He went into the kitchen, where Aunt Lily was cooking dinner.

"Hey, Eddie!" she said. "How's it going?"

"It's going okay, I guess. Busy. A lot of work. I have to work a lot harder to get the same grades here as I did at OHS."

"Mmmm. Hear anything else from your mom?"

Ugh. Why did he have to even come in here? Stupid. He didn't want to talk about his mom. Every time he thought he had something regular to think about, like too much work or Tanya or whatever, she came back up.

"No. I sent her a card, but I haven't heard anything."

"Well, she called here today. She's gotten far enough along that I guess they are allowing her phone calls. She wanted to check up on you. I told her you were doing great. I wasn't lying, was I?"

"No! I mean, no. I'm doing great. I mean, I really like school, and I . . . well, it's just nice to have fun, you know? I never had much fun while Mom was . . . after Dad died."

Aunt Lily quietly eyed him. Eddie cursed himself. Ugh! Why did he even say that? Well, Aunt Lily wanted something, and Eddie felt like he had to give her something. He really did feel grateful for being able to live here and be a lot more like a normal kid than he had been since Dad died. "Do you think that talking to Don is helping?" Aunt Lily asked.

"Honestly?" Eddie asked.

"Yeah." Aunt Lily smiled. "Honestly."

"I always feel worse every Wednesday night. And we talk about the same stuff over and over. I don't want to be . . . I mean, I know . . . I don't want to sound ungrateful or anything. It just feels kind of pointless."

Aunt Lily chopped something for a minute. "Well, maybe we'll think about some other options. Do you think it would be better to be with a group?"

Eddie thought about that. It might actually be nice to meet some other kids whose parents were screwed up, so he wouldn't feel like he was the only one. "I dunno. Maybe."

"I'll look into it. Listen, you know your mom's going to be done pretty soon, right?"

"What?" Eddie barked. He had known that his mom was going to get out of rehab at some point, but since he hadn't been exactly counting the days, and since he didn't know how many days the program lasted anyway, counting the days wouldn't have made much sense.

"I thought you'd be happy," Aunt Lily said, like she was really puzzled.

"Uh, well, I mean, yeah, I'm happy for her if she's better. I mean, of course I'm happy," Eddie said, but then why did he feel like punching something? Maybe because he liked his life, he liked living here, weird food and all, he liked the way Alex made him laugh and had his back and was his friend. The idea of returning to Oldham with Mom seemed like falling into a deep, dark hole that he'd probably never be able to climb out of. He thought about reminding Aunt Lily that she'd said he could stay here as long as he needed, of begging her to keep him here even if Mom was out of rehab, but that would be a long Meaningful Talk, and he couldn't do that right now.

The phone rang, and Eddie practically sprinted across the room to answer it, knowing it wasn't for him, but hoping that the distraction would bring an end to this conversation.

Strangely enough, it was for him. It was Savon. "Hey, Left Eye."

"Soap!" Eddie said gratefully. "What's up?"

"I just got the preliminary Web page design done. Take a look." He gave Eddie the address.

"Hang on, hang on, I gotta get to the computer here." He signaled to Aunt Lily that he had to take the phone, and she nodded and smiled. He hoped he could avoid finishing their conversation.

He pulled up the site, which Savon had paid for with his own money. "Whoa, Savon, it looks fantastic! How did you get that subway train to go across the front like that?"

"Don't laugh, okay?"

"Yeah, okay, what?"

"I've been studying HTML and Java for like three years. So, you know, that's the only reason you could beat me at Madden. It cuts into my Madden time."

"Well, I was doing all the shopping and the laundry for a whole year, and I still beat you." He said this before he even realized what he was saying, before he could stop himself from saying too much. Aunt Lily had messed up his head with thoughts of his mom, and he forgot to be careful. Or maybe he'd gotten so comfortable in his new life that he'd just forgotten that he had to hide the old one.

There was a pause, and Eddie's heart pounded as he thought, Please don't ask, please don't ask. Savon finally said, "So you keeping Alex in check? Is he doing anything?"

"Kenisha's keeping him in check this week. They went to Blue Hill Ave. today, they're going someplace called Dudley Downs or something next week."

"It's just Dudley, Left Eye. They're going down Dudley. Dudley Square."

"Oh. Right. Anyway, even if he's not doing anything, Kenisha is there, so something will get done."

"What about you and Tanya?"

"We're going to Jamison Creative on Thursday."

"Okay, then. Just make sure you get some work done. You know, don't just sit there droolin'."

"Oh, I'm all about getting the work done. I don't, I mean, I'm not—"

"Yeah, yeah, whatever. Don't front."

Eddie smiled and said, as whitely as he could, "Yes, I will now discontinue my fronting. I sincerely hope to hit that."

Savon gave a big laugh that lasted a long time. "You and everybody else at school," he said.

"Ah, but as you may or may not be aware, I am the mack. Kelvin pronounced it so."

Savon laughed again. "Yeah, well, if you start believing everything Kelvin says, you in some trouble."

Eddie laughed, and they hung up. He headed to his room to brainstorm marketing ideas—and avoid Aunt Lily.

At about seven-thirty, Eddie heard Alex come home. "Attention! Attention please! All denizens of unit three kindly bow down to the master salesman!" Alex bellowed as he walked in.

"All right, Alex, calm down, will you?" Aunt Lily said. Eddie headed toward the kitchen. It was safe now that Alex was home, and anyway he was starving.

"Hey, Lily, you look great today. Order us up some food, will ya? I think it's going to be a long night on this project. Thanks, hon, you're doing a great job." Alex was clearly so high on himself that he had lost his mind.

Eddie entered the kitchen as Aunt Lily laughed and said, "Listen, mister, I don't know who convinced you I'm your assistant, but you'll be washing dishes until you retire if you try that again!"

Alex smiled. "Edward! Ask me how many businesses we sold on the Boston Teen Traffic idea this afternoon!"

"Hey, Alexander, how many businesses did you sell on the Boston Teen Traffic idea this afternoon?"

"Eight, my friend. Eight. This for a service that doesn't even exist. Mother, forgive my earlier arrogance. I am going to pull a grade on this project that will at last make you proud of me."

"You know I'm proud of you already, Alex. Dad's going to be late, so let's sit and eat something."

They all got plates, and Aunt Lily heaped them high with some kind of stew on some tiny rice things. Eddie dug in. He was so hungry that he barely noticed the weird spices—he just devoured it. After he'd had a few bites, he said, "So Savon called and showed me the Web site. It looks fantastic."

"Hey, that's awesome," Alex replied. "So it seems that the sales force is doing a great job, the Web designer is doing a great job, which leaves the marketing team. I hope you don't get too, uh, distracted while working with the lovely—ow! Damn!" Eddie had kicked him hard under the table. He did not want to talk about Tanya with Aunt Lily. Please don't let her ask, please don't let her ask . . .

Aunt Lily raised an eyebrow, looked from Eddie to Alex and back to Eddie. She looked like she might open her mouth, but instead she smiled.

Eddie thought he'd gotten away from that one pretty easily, but he had to get a little revenge. "So, um, Alex, stopped off for any *Vietnamese food* lately?"

Aunt Lily looked at them quizzically and raised an eyebrow again. Alex was smooth, though, and came back with "I think I may be losing my taste for that particular cuisine. It doesn't seem to be agreeing with me lately."

Eddie smiled, and Aunt Lily again looked like she was about to speak, but she said nothing, and they eventually talked about other stuff.

After dinner Eddie and Alex washed dishes, and Eddie kept sneaking glances at the clock.

"She said after eight, Eddie," Alex said, "which does not mean you should call her at 8:13. It's gonna look desperate."

"I'm only calling about the project," Eddie answered. "Aggh. What am I going to say?"

"Tell her when your appointment is for, and tell her if you have any . . . creative ideas." Alex said this last part like it was the dirtiest thing in the world. "I mean, I'll bet you have a lot of . . . creative ideas you'd just love to share."

Eddie laughed, decided he couldn't win this one, and dried a plate.

At 8:34 he couldn't stand it anymore and picked up the phone to call Tanya. As it rang, his heart pounded in his chest, and he kept thinking, Please let it be voice mail, please let it be voice mail . . .

"Hello?"

"Uh, um, hi, yeah, Tanya, it's Eddie calling."

"Left Eye! My boy! What's up?"

"I made us an appointment at Jamison for Thursday afternoon, so if you can get off work then . . ."

"Yeah, no problem. But what are we gonna create up in the Jamison Creative, Left Eye?"

"Well, I've been working on a few ideas, I think we should go over together—"

"All right, all right, look, I'm mad busy, but let's have lunch on Monday and go over stuff so we don't walk in there looking stupid, then get lectures from Lewis, all 'my former colleagues inform me that your level of preparation, blah blah blah.' "

Eddie laughed. That was the exact speech Lewis had given in class yesterday after another group showed up at Jamison Creative and apparently expected the Jamison people to come up with their ideas for them and not just show them how to use the equipment. "Okay, see you Monday, then," he said.

"Okay, bye," Tanya said.

Eddie hadn't noticed, but Alex was right by his side. "So?" he said.

"So we're having lunch on Monday," Eddie said, smiling. Alex started saying something, but Eddie didn't listen. He was lost in thought, trying to work out scenarios where this lunch became something more than just a lunch, where Tanya made it clear that somebody who looked as good as her actually did want to date somebody like him, where he knew what to say.

He also realized he had to come up with some ideas so he didn't look like a complete idiot on Monday. He fell asleep trying to write ads for the sides of buses.

Eddie's morning classes on Monday were a complete blur. In his mind, he was already eating lunch with Tanya, and impressing her with his wit and intelligence, or at least his intelligence. Finally it was time for lunch, and Eddie met Tanya in the hall.

"So where should we go for our big date?" Tanya said, smiling. Was she trying to make him nervous?

"Uh, I don't know," he stammered, "I usually bring my lunch, so . . ."

"Okay, then, let's go around the corner to Bulger Brothers Burgers."

"Uh, okay." They crammed into an elevator with about fifteen other kids and walked in silence to the burger place. With every step Eddie tried to think of something to say, but he eventually figured that saying nothing was better than saying something stupid.

When they got to the burger place, Eddie looked around and saw the juicy, dripping burgers that all the downtown office workers were eating. The guys had their ties over their shoulders and had tucked big napkins into their collars. They looked incredibly dumb, but probably not as dumb as they might look with burger grease, ketchup, and mayo all over their shirts. Eddie figured there was no way he could eat something that messy in front of Tanya. He had nearly decided to get just fries when he heard Tanya order a cheeseburger with everything, so now he pretty much had to get at least that much so he didn't look girly. Plus, the burgers smelled really good.

Once they got their food, Eddie flung his tie over his shoulder, bent gingerly over his plate, and tried to eat without slopping juice on himself.

Tanya took big, hungry bites, and when a little drop of ketchup dripped on the front of her shirt and she started dabbing it with a napkin, Eddie really thought his brain might explode. Finally he said, "So, what kind of stuff have you come up with?"

"You go ahead and go first," Tanya said between bites. Eddie wondered if she had anything, or if she was just expecting him to do all the work. Which would actually be fine if it led to her thinking of him as more than a friend.

"Well, obviously we have to get people's attention in the places where our customers are. I was thinking, um, I mean, well, I thought if we just made up some stickers with the Web address and some kind of catchy line or something, we could stick them everywhere. We can ask the Jamison guys, but I think we could get maybe ten thousand stickers printed for not very much money . . ." He looked at Tanya, who smiled at him and nodded.

"And then once we sort of get people's attention with that, we could go to ads on the buses and trains. I called the T for the rates, and I think the prices can work for us if we actually sign up as many advertisers as Alex seems to think we can."

"That sounds great, Left Eye," Tanya said, smiling. She wiped her chin and said, "Okay, well, I gotta bounce, you know, get my homework together before class and whatnot. So Thursday, right after school, right?"

"Yeah. I told the Jamison people we'd be over there by four-fifteen."

"Great. Thanks!" and she was gone. Eddie looked at his watch and saw that there was still fifteen minutes of lunch period left. That was good, because he'd only eaten half his lunch. Why hadn't she stayed? Well, she did call it a date, and she did smile at him a lot. Maybe she really was busy.

18

ALEX GOT A TEXT MESSAGE THE
next day during English that said, "MLVLS 4PM?—HNH."
He fumbled with his phone under the table, hoping he didn't
get caught and get his phone confiscated again, because Dad
had told him he wasn't coming down here to retrieve his
phone from discipline hock again, and he could just buy himself another one if this one was taken away. "OK," he sent, and
quickly put the phone back in his pocket. Everybody was paying attention to Kelvin, who was saying, "I actually think the
witches are responsible for Macbeth's actions. Because if they
hadn't said anything, he never would have even thought of
murdering Duncan." The perfect crime!

He spent the rest of the afternoon preparing to get
dumped. He could just tell it was coming. He didn't really
know why, although a couple of times Kenisha had acted like
she was about to say something to him, which Alex was sure

was going to be a warning that he was on the express train to dumpsville. He tried to think of reasons why he was glad he was going to get dumped, but all he could come up with was if Hanh was nuts enough to break up with him for no reason, he was better off.

He considered trying to break up with her, but he couldn't really think of a good reason to, and besides, he was kind of curious to know why she wanted to dump him, and he wanted to hear her say it. If he initiated the breakup, he'd have the advantage, but he would also let her out of doing all the hard stuff.

So when four o'clock came, he walked into Melville's and saw that there was a new hot girl with tattoos working there. He kind of wondered if they kept a supply of them in the back where they kept the milk and sugar and stuff, and every so often the manager would call back, like, "Hey, tattooed hottie out front!"

Hanh was already sitting. She had managed to snag the two plush chairs in the front window, which was an amazing feat. Well, Alex thought, at least I'll be comfortable while I'm getting dumped.

He sat down without bending over to kiss or hug her. He decided not to even bother with the small talk, so he said, smiling, "You're dumping me."

Hanh furrowed her brow. "Did Kenisha tell you? Because she—"

"No, it's just obvious. You got all funny all the sudden. I don't need Kenisha to tell me that."

"Well, I was going to put it more nicely than that, but yeah, Alex, I want to break up."

"Do I get to know why, or is this just one of those mystery things? Is it like your dad doesn't want you dating a white guy or something?"

"No, dummy. I can date whoever I want. Just not you."

Ouch. Alex was trying to get the upper hand here, and instead he got his butt handed to him. "I mean, no, that sounds awful, I mean, I like you, Alex, I really do, but I'm mad busy with work and stuff, and I have to keep my grades up, and they have been slipping lately."

"So what? My grades never really had anywhere to slip to."

"Yeah, but your parents don't work fourteen hours a day, Alex. I am not about staying in that restaurant my whole life, and if I am going to go to college and have my parents be proud of me and everything, I have to focus on school."

"But why can't you . . ." Uh-oh. Alex stopped himself in mid-sentence because he realized he might have been about to beg, which was not happening.

"I mean, I could probably have a boyfriend, Alex, but, you know, no offense, not you. I mean, you ain't serious, and it's mad hard for me to do everything I do, keeping up on my work, helping out at the restaurant, and I can't be spending my time with somebody who makes me want to slack off. I want to be lazy, I really do, I want to not go home some nights, I want to go out and have fun, but I can't. And I can't spend my time with somebody who's living that way, because if I go that way, it's gonna have serious consequences for me."

Mom, Dad, Harrison, Lewis, Eddie, and now Hanh. Alex is selfish and lazy. He was tired of hearing it, but nobody seemed to be tired of saying it. "Okay, then. Are we done here?"

"Please don't be like that, Alex."

"Well, you know me, I'm lazy and selfish and I don't want to spend any time doing something I don't want to do, and listening to you I guess falls into that category right now." Maybe that was too mean, but the hell with it. Who was she to tell him he was lazy? He'd busted his butt on Blue Hill Ave. the other day, doing all the talking while Kenisha just stood there, not like somebody that shy could talk to these guys who ran the shops, no, that was all Alex, putting his charm and his intelligence to work, and so what if he liked having fun? On what planet was that a bad thing?

"Fine," she said, and gathered up her stuff and left without saying goodbye.

Alex put his feet up on the little table in front of the comfy chair and sipped his latte. "Hey, kid, you can't do that," the tattooed barista said from behind the counter.

"I just got dumped here. You wanna give me a break?"

"Tell you what," she said, reaching behind the counter and grabbing a biscotti, which she tossed at him. He grabbed it as she continued, "Free biscotti for anybody who gets dumped on the premises. Now put your feet down."

He smiled. Free baked goods from a sexy older woman! "Deal!" he said.

When he got home that afternoon, Dad was waiting at the elevator. "Hey." Alex greeted him without much enthusiasm. He was trying to focus on the future and all the other girls he could still go out with, but he couldn't help being mad at

Hanh. Not so much because she broke up with him, but because she got all high-and-mighty on him. Yeah, God forbid you should have some fun and make out in the stairwell once in a while. Alex just wanted to enjoy life, and he couldn't understand why everybody had a problem with that.

"Listen, Alex. I think maybe you should talk to Eddie. He . . . uh, he had a bad day."

"Yeah, well, my day wasn't so hot either, Dad, thanks for asking, though."

"Don't be a smart-ass, Alex. Eddie's mom called him today. Mom was pretty upset, too, and she tried to talk to him, but he won't talk to her."

"Maybe he doesn't want to talk about it! Did that occur to any of you geniuses? Do you ever see him on Wednesday nights? Maybe talking about it isn't always such a great idea!"

"I see you're obviously feeling too selfish right now to think about anybody else, so forget I asked, okay?"

Alex was so angry he wanted to punch something. He did care about Eddie, but he knew enough to know that when Eddie was feeling bad, he didn't want fourteen adults coming up to him all "How are you feeling, let's talk about it." Alex was upset, too, and he didn't want to talk to his mom about it either.

In their bedroom, Alex found Eddie sitting on his bed, staring at the wall.

"Hey," he said.

"Hey," Eddie answered.

Alex lay down on his own bed and stared at the ceiling for a while. "So," he finally said.

"Yeah?" Eddie answered.

"I had a crappy day. What about you?"

"Yeah. Crappy."

"Let's go to the movies."

"Okay."

"I'll call everybody. What do you wanna see?"

"I don't care. No, something where a lot of people die, where stuff blows up, where there's blood and big guns and death."

"That sounds good to me, too." Alex called Savon, who asked if he could bring Deshawn, and then Kelvin, and then went and told his parents that he was taking Eddie to the movies.

As they sat on the bus heading downtown, Eddie said quietly, "She wants me back. When she gets out. She wants us to start over."

"Uh . . . oh. Sorry, I guess."

"Yeah, I want to tell her I already started over without her, but I guess you can't say that to your mom. I mean, I don't know, your mom did tell me I could stay with you guys as long as I needed to, but I don't think she meant even if my mom wants me back."

"I don't know. Mom's . . . I think she'd fight with Aunt Dinah if she felt like that was best for you." And then, before he could stop to think how embarrassing it would sound, Alex added, "I hope you get to stay." Which was his way of saying "I care about you, and I even like hanging out with you, and it's actually fun having another kid in the house," but of course he couldn't say any of that stuff.

"Thanks," Eddie said. "Me too." And Alex knew he meant that he heard everything Alex didn't say, and that he had some stuff he wasn't saying, too.

"Well," Alex said brightly, "in other news, I got dumped today."

"Sorry."

"Yeah, but it frees me up for all the other ladies who are always sweatin' me." Alex smiled, trying to make himself forget how mad and hurt he was.

Eddie laughed. "Yeah, time to open up the waiting list, huh?"

They met Savon and Deshawn and Kelvin at the movies and bought tickets for something rated PG and then snuck into some action movie where people got their limbs hacked off and girls took their shirts off for no reason. Everybody agreed it was pretty good.

"Yo, that movie was off the chains!" Kelvin said as they emerged.

"Yes," Eddie said in his new extra-white voice he used in these kinds of situations, which Alex had to admit was better than trying to pull off some slang he just couldn't do. "The film certainly was not on any chains, or, indeed, hooks."

"Shut up, Left Eye," Kelvin said, and then said, "Oh, snap! Check out Tanya! And check out the other two!"

Yes, there in the lobby stood Tanya, who was most certainly pushing the boundaries of professional attire, and two girls who were even hotter than her.

"Whoa . . ." Savon said quietly, and all five boys stood there stunned for a moment.

Kelvin regained his composure first and called out,
"Yo, 212!"

Tanya saw them and grimaced. Alex noticed that Eddie was
looking all over the lobby, trying but failing to act casual. "Oh
no!" Tanya said. "It's those fools. And my boy Left Eye, of
course. Can't dis my project partner." Yeah, Alex thought, especially when he's going to do all the work for you.

Tanya and her two friends whispered, smiled, and walked
over. "This is my cousin Stephanie and my friend Kendra,"
Tanya said.

There was a moment of silence, and Alex realized that they
were all just standing there drooling, so he had to step in. "So,
we're about to head down to Faneuil Hall, get some ice cream,
make fun of the tourists, that kind of thing. You ladies care to
join us?"

There was more whispering, peeking (was Stephanie peeking at him?), and smiling, at least by Stephanie and Kendra.
Tanya, Alex noticed, was pretty much rolling her eyes and
shaking her head. She bent over to hear something Kendra
was saying to her, then turned to the boys and said, "Okay. But
you fools start crackin' on us, we're gonna steal on all of y'all,
and you know three of us can take five of you without even
breaking a sweat."

"I don't know," Kelvin said, "look to me like y'all are sweatin'
me already."

Tanya raised a fist and swung halfheartedly at Kelvin, who
was running away, and they started walking toward Faneuil
Hall.

At first they walked in two groups, but as they walked, the

groups started merging into one. After about five minutes, Alex found himself walking next to Tanya, who was walking next to Eddie.

"So," Tanya said, "what movie did y'all see?"

"*Court of Blood,*" Alex answered. "What about you?"

"We seen *My Prince Charming.* It was mad corny."

"Yeah, Eddie wanted us to see that, but we had to say no way," Alex said, trying to steer the conversation over to Eddie, who was walking over there looking like some kind of fish, opening his mouth and then closing it, trying so hard not to be shy it kind of made Alex sad and uncomfortable to watch it. Anyway, he noticed that Kelvin was monopolizing Stephanie, while Savon and Deshawn were all over Kendra, and Alex was thinking that Stephanie might be an ideal replacement for Hanh and was pretty sure that he could outtalk Kelvin, though Kelvin did have the height and looks over him.

"I did not want to see that. I had to pull you out of line for *Love and Menopause,*" Eddie said, and Alex had to give it to him, he was getting much better at this.

"Well, I heard Kelvin's mom was in that, and you know how I like them older women," Alex replied.

As he predicted, this remark pulled Kelvin's attention away from Stephanie, and he was able to join that little group by insisting that yes, he did have beef, and yes, he would be happy to go right here if Kelvin thought he was man enough. This was a double win, because it got him over to Stephanie and left Tanya and Eddie alone to talk about whatever they might talk about.

He still wasn't sure if the match was a good idea, but he figured he hadn't really expected to like Eddie that much at first, but there was something about the kid that definitely grew on you, and maybe he'd grow on Tanya the same way.

As they got their ice cream, Alex found himself next to Tanya in line, but he made sure he got the seat next to Stephanie that Kelvin wanted. Tanya sat on the other side of him, and Eddie sat on the other side of her. Alex made Stephanie laugh three times, which was a good start, and eventually he got her to give up her phone number, which he hoped he had gotten into his phone right, but he wasn't sure because Tanya bumped into him while he was putting the number in.

Finally Eddie leaned over Tanya, stealing a quick glance down at her chest as he did so (my boy! Alex thought), and said, "Uh, hey, Alex, what time did you tell your folks we'd be home?"

"Ten—oh, snap!" It was nearly nine-forty. "Time to bounce! Bye, everybody!" Alex called out. He and Eddie walked until they got out of everyone else's sight, then ran for five minutes to the bus stop, then stood there for two minutes cursing (well, Alex did most of the cursing, while Eddie just kind of stood there) until the bus came.

The bus came at 9:47, and Alex knew they'd be home on time. As they flopped down in the seats, Alex said, "Okay, we're gonna make it. And I got digits. A good night. How about you?"

Eddie was silent for a minute, then said, "I already have Tanya's digits. We had a really nice talk, but I don't know if it means anything." He paused. "She looks even better when she's not in her professional attire, huh?"

"You got that right."

"Yeah."

Tired and content, they both smiled.

19

EDDIE HAD A VERY HARD TIME falling asleep that night, and he spent Wednesday in a kind of daze with three thoughts cycling through his mind over and over. One, of course, was Mom. He wished he could get her voice out of his head, but he just kept hearing it: "We're going to be a family again, Eddie, I promise." He had had no idea what to say to that. "I've heard your promises before"? "Great, when do you get here"? "It's too late"? That was what he'd wanted to say, but instead he'd settled for "I'm glad."

When he'd come to stay here, her rehab stint seemed like it would last forever, but now it had been two months and she was almost out, and maybe she'd gotten better and maybe she hadn't. Eddie had looked on the Internet and found that even the very best programs have at least half of their participants relapse. Eddie did not want to be around the first time Mom got fired, or dumped, or whatever, and decided that she needed a little something to take the edge off. He'd seen that movie too many times. And even if she was better, how could he go back to Oldham now? He felt like he'd left that guy—the lonely scared overachiever—back in Oldham, and he was afraid he'd become that guy again if he went back. He hated that guy.

And then there was Tanya. It was just impossible to figure her out. She didn't exactly make it obvious if she liked him. But what about all that stuff she said? "My brother's in the Marines and I'm mad scared for him." "I think maybe my dad drinks too much." Girls didn't just tell that kind of stuff to anybody, did they? If a girl, especially one as tough as Tanya, was telling you she was mad scared about anything, didn't that mean she liked you? If she trusted you that much, wouldn't she want to be your girlfriend?

Alex called Stephanie and talked to her for forty-five minutes on Wednesday night, and Eddie, worn out from therapy, wanted an excuse to call Tanya. He also wished this could be as easy for him as it was for Alex. Eddie had joked about the waiting list, but he had to hand it to Alex: he didn't sit around moping about the girl who *didn't* like him—he got out there and started talking to girls who *might* like him. It was just easy for Alex to talk to girls. Eddie always found it easy to listen to girls, but somehow he knew it wasn't the same thing.

When he wasn't worrying about his mom or Tanya, Eddie tried to think about what they were going to create at Jamison Creative tomorrow. He figured they should keep it simple, and have the bus ads be the same as the stickers. But what should they say? Eddie was so distracted by Tanya that he didn't seem to have any good ideas.

He finally gave in and called Tanya with the flimsy excuse of reminding her about their appointment at Jamison Creative. His heart thudded in his chest as the phone rang, and he wanted to hang up but found his hand wouldn't let him, so he just prayed he'd get voice mail, but then she picked up on the fourth ring.

"Hello?"

"Uh, hi, Tanya, it's Eddie."

"Left Eye! What's up?"

"I wanted to remind you about tomorrow, I mean not that I think you'd forget, but I kind of have to make doubly sure because you know Lewis would freak out if anything went wrong."

"I see, gotta keep me in check, huh? Make sure I do some work?"

"No, I just—"

"That's cool, I know I need it. I got you for tomorrow, though. I took time off work and everything."

"Great!" What now? Was there any way to keep this conversation going? Should he ask about her brother? Would that be annoying? He knew damn well he shouldn't ask about her dad: that would violate the Addicts' Kids Code. Two seconds that felt like about twenty years ticked by as Eddie fumbled for something to say. Finally he came up with "Okay, then, I guess I'll see you tomorrow. Bring all your best ideas!" Ugh. Lame lame lame.

"Yeah, well, I bet my best ideas won't be as good as your worst ones, but okay, I'll see you tomorrow." They said goodbye and hung up, and Eddie smiled.

Thursday was another foggy day. Everybody was still making fun of Tanya in advisory—"Yo, how somebody as ugly as you got a cousin so fine?" and "Yo, Kendra was mad nice—why she hang with you?"—and Eddie figured he could either make fun of Tanya, too, which would be playing it cool, or else turn it around and make fun of how everybody had been standing there with their tongues hanging out, which Tanya might appreciate. Then again, he'd had his tongue hanging out, and he didn't need Kelvin pointing that out. So he pretended to study and hoped to stay out of it. Of course, this was impossible, and Kelvin started quizzing Tanya about how she'd been sitting and walking next to Eddie all night. Fortunately, Kenisha interrupted Kelvin with "Could you just stop talking for five minutes so I can do this equation? Damn!"

Everybody looked at her and then got quiet. Kenisha never talked in advisory, she certainly never swore, and she had never seemed to be bothered by people talking before. Eddie guessed that, like everybody else, she was stressed out from eating, breathing, and sleeping the marketing project. He was glad, because it saved him from Kelvin and everybody else messing with him when he was already nervous about working with Tanya this afternoon.

Four o'clock finally came. Eddie walked into another high-rise tower and looked around the lobby for Tanya. He didn't

see her, so he signed in with the security guard and took the
elevator to the offices of Jamison Creative on the eighteenth
floor. He hadn't seen Tanya's name on the sign-in log, and he
wondered if he should wait for her, but then they'd both be
late, and Lewis would go on about unprofessional behavior
and *my former colleagues blah blah blah.* Of course, he might
do that anyway if they didn't arrive together, but Eddie liked
his chances better this way.

He spoke to the receptionist, who informed him that Mr.
Wu would be with him shortly. Tanya arrived before he could
even have a seat on the dark red leather couch with shiny
metal arms and legs.

"Yo, Left Eye, sorry I'm late! I hope Lewis don't kill us!"

"Well, you only got here like thirty seconds after me, and
Mr. Wu hasn't come out yet, so I think we're safe."

They waited for another five minutes, and Mr. Wu finally
came out, greeted them, mentioned that he was a graduate of
Boston Public Schools and he was excited to be helping them.
He was an Asian guy in his twenties who had the sleeves of his
white oxford rolled up. He took them to a conference room
and asked them what they'd need for their project. Tanya
looked at Eddie, who said, "Well, I think we're going for the
print stuff—we'd like some sticker ads and then bigger ver-
sions of the same thing for the T and the buses."

"Okay!" Mr. Wu said. "So it sounds like what you need for
today is a little bit of training on the graphic design software,
which is good—it's pretty intuitive, and actually kind of fun
to put stuff together with it."

"Excellent. Thanks!"

Mr. Wu spent an hour showing them how to work the software. Eddie took notes, and Tanya listened, but didn't write anything down. Eddie hoped Mr. Wu didn't notice, because he was pretty sure they'd lose points if Lewis got some kind of report about how not everybody in the group was participating.

Mr. Wu left, and there they were, alone in this office which was kind of dark, probably so you could see the big computer screen better, but whatever, it was dark and Tanya was right next to him. She smelled really good, and it was getting really hard for Eddie to think about making ads when all the blood in his body seemed to be running away from his brain.

Eddie said, "Um, I had a couple of ideas, but I don't want to, you know, take over everything or whatever."

"It's cool. What do you got?"

"Well, I thought for the stickers we could have a real simple slogan—something that will make people curious—and then the Web address so they can find out what it's all about. Maybe we can figure out a cool font or something, and then we should think about colors—even just two colors will catch more attention and look better than those black-and-white stickers people make in their basements."

"Okay. That sounds good." Tanya suddenly dug her phone out of her pocket and answered it. Eddie guessed it was probably on vibrate. "Yeah. Yeah? No, I'm in the middle . . . yeah. No, I can't yo, this is a really bad time, I got this project. No, I *have to*. It's my *grade*. Yeah, fine. Tanya will take care of it. *Again* . . . okay. Yeah. Okay, okay."

She hung up the phone and laid a hand on Eddie's arm.

"Okay, so it turns out I got a situation here I need to go deal with." What kind of situation? Eddie wondered. A boyfriend situation? A brother situation? A drunk dad situation?

"So I'll be back in fifteen minutes, okay? I'm sorry, Eddie, you know I wouldn't do this to you if I didn't have to . . ." She was calling him Eddie now, instead of Left Eye. Was that good?

"It's all right. I'll just get started, and then maybe you can do the second shift."

"Thanks, Eddie. You're the bomb." She ruffled his hair as she said that, and he felt like telling her she could take hours if she needed to. As it turned out, he should have told her that, because an hour later, after Mr. Wu had checked on him for the third time and raised his eyebrows at Tanya's absence, Eddie was starving and was just printing out his sticker designs (they said YOU GOT BEEF? in big red letters with the Web address in blue underneath, or else YO SHORTY, WHY YOU WALKIN' AWAY FOR? in blue with the Web address in red) when Tanya finally came back.

"Yo, I am so sorry, Eddie. I had no idea it was . . . Well, anyway, that took longer than I thought it would."

"It's okay," Eddie said, and he almost meant it. He did, after all, know a lot about having situations in your life. Still, it would have been nice to be able to talk about the slogans with Tanya before the sticker designs had to get done. He thought maybe the slogans were kind of dumb and didn't really have anything to do with getting to school safely, except that those were things he figured people might say to you if they were messing with you, and he hoped they'd make people curious enough to check the site. More important, if Tanya had started on the bus ads when he started on the stickers, they'd be finished with their work at Jamison Creative already.

"Yo, these look great! I could see sticking these on every pole in the neighborhood! What do we have to do?"

"Well, I guess we can just resize this stuff for the design for the bus ads and then get something printed and we'll be done," he said.

"Oh, good," Tanya said, " 'cause I really need to get myself home soon." Okay, Eddie thought, I'll just go ahead and do that because it would take me three times as long to show you how to do this stuff because you weren't listening and haven't touched the software yet, and I wouldn't mind spending all night here with you, but maybe you'll be grateful if I help you get home earlier.

Eddie worked in silence for the next few minutes, enjoying the way Tanya smelled, enjoying sitting in a dark room with just her, enjoying being good at something in front of her.

When the bus ad designs were printed, Tanya said again how good they were and gave Eddie a big hug. A full-press hug. He blushed and hoped she hadn't noticed exactly how excited that hug made him while it was going on. He tried to adjust his pants and sat back down.

"Hey, Eddie, before we go let me ask you something," Tanya said.

Eddie couldn't hear himself squeak out "Okay" over the pounding of his heart, but he guessed he must have said it, because Tanya leaned a little closer to him, still smelling fantastic, and said, "You know, this ain't something I would normally do, but you're mad cool, you know." Oh my God, Eddie thought, she's going to kiss me, she's going to kiss me right here in the offices of Jamison Creative, and Mr. Wu is going to check on us, and Lewis is going to yell at us about how "making out in the office does not constitute professional behavior," and maybe we'll even get suspended. It'll totally be worth it.

But she wasn't kissing him. She was still talking, and Eddie was pretty sure she had just said something about how she could really talk to him, and she thought of him like a brother or something. Eddie didn't know much about girls, but he knew enough to know that most of them did not make out with their brothers. His heart that had been pounding so loudly suddenly sank into his shoes.

"This is mad embarrassing, but I know I can trust you to keep it on the DL, you know, 'cause you and me are cool like that. So, you know, do you think maybe Alex would go out with me?"

Well, this was a pretty ugly turn of events. Eddie had no idea how to answer that question, because all he wanted to say was "Why the hell did you hug me? Why did you tell me all that stuff about your life? I don't want to be cool like that, I want to be uncool like Alex, who I can't believe you like, except I can because he can pretty much have any girl he wants, and I did all the work for you like a sucker and you were *playing* me, I'm pretty sure is what Savon would call it."

Unable to speak, Eddie quickly gathered up his stuff. Tanya stared at him. "Uh . . . Eddie? Did you hear me?"

He had to get out of this office. "Um, yeah, well, Tanya, I

think Alex would go out with just about anybody," he said, and walked as fast as he could to the elevator without even thanking Mr. Wu, which would probably get him in trouble on top of everything else.

Once he was inside the elevator with the doors closed, Eddie was so mad and so embarrassed that he felt like he might explode. He kicked the side of the elevator. Hard. It hurt his toe.

20

ALEX WAS ON THE PHONE WITH
Stephanie when his call-waiting beeped. He looked at the
phone, saw it was a restricted number, and almost blew it off,
but then he got a weird feeling like he should answer it. Eddie
still wasn't back from Jamison Creative, and while Alex
thought he could probably handle himself on the T, there was
always the possibility that he was injured and calling from a
pay phone near the bus stop or something. He told Stephanie
that Eddie needed some help getting his project stuff out of
the elevator, and he'd call her back.

"Hello?"

"Hey. It's Eddie."

"Eddie, where are you? It's getting late, and while Dad is
cool with holding dinner, I think you should try to get home
soon."

"I'm not hungry. You guys go ahead and eat. I'm just calling to let you know I'm okay, I'll be home soon," Eddie said, but his voice didn't really sound all that okay.

"Where are you?"

"I'm hanging out with the only female I will apparently ever get to see naked, which is our friend at the library. I'm on a pay phone."

"Okay. Did something happen with your mom?"

"You know, for once it has nothing to do with Mom. I just feel stupid. Tanya disappeared while I did all the work and then came back and told me she thought of me like a brother and she liked somebody else."

"Oh, man. I'm sorry. Thinks of you like a brother. You gotta hate that. Ouch. I can't believe she did that to you. I'm gonna have to regulate on her," he said, hoping that the unlikely image of him trying to regulate on anybody, much less Tanya, who could definitely wreck him, would get a laugh out of Eddie.

It didn't.

"Well, you might want to hold off on the regulation, because then she might not like you anymore," Eddie said, and he hung up the phone.

Great. This was going to screw everything up. What was he going to do now? His big plan to help Eddie blew up in his face. If he hadn't tried to stick Eddie and Tanya together . . . well, but he had. He supposed that would teach him to try to be unselfish. It only got you trouble.

Alex told Mom and Dad that Eddie was working late on the project, and then he sat down to eat something gross that involved truffle oil, or so Dad kept telling him.

After dinner, he finished his homework and decided to play video games for a while. He was on the verge of finally beating the boss at the end of the fourth level when the phone rang. It was the house phone and not his cell phone, but Eddie still wasn't home, and so Alex decided he'd better answer it before Dad got it in case Eddie needed him to cover for him.

He picked up the phone and said hello as the elevator opened and Eddie walked in.

"Sweetie, I'm so glad to finally talk to you! How are you doing?" Aunt Dinah said on the other end of the phone.

"Uh . . . I . . ." Alex muttered.

"It's okay, sweetie, I know it's hard to talk to me, believe me I do know, and I know I already said I was sorry, but . . ." and she started to cry and kind of squeaked the rest out, "just hearing your voice makes me . . ." And she dissolved into tears.

Well, hell, Alex thought, I sure get stuck with some unpleasant stuff for somebody who's supposedly famous for being selfish. Should he hand the phone over to Eddie?

He waited until there was a little break and then said, "Aunt Dinah, um, this is actually Alex. Eddie is—" and as he said this, Eddie started making these big, cartoonish gestures trying to say no, he wasn't here, he didn't want to talk to his mom, lie for me please, Alex, lie for me, you owe me that much after the girl I like just told me she liked you.

Actually, that last part was probably only Alex's guilty conscience, even though he didn't really have any reason to feel guilty. Still, he knew Eddie had had a tough day, and they had to look out for each other. "Eddie is still out working on our big marketing project. Um, do you want me to tell him any-thing?"

"Oh Jesus Christ, I'm sorry, Alex, you probably want to hear me crying even less than Eddie does. I'm sorry, kiddo."

"Don't worry about it. It's okay. So, anyway."

"Right. Tell him that I love him very much, and I can't wait to see him, and things are going to be different."

"Okay. I'll tell him."

"Thanks, Alex. How's he doing, anyway?"

"Good, I guess. He's getting better grades than me, but you probably could've guessed that. But, yeah, he's doing great. Really great." Even though he'd said Eddie was great, he didn't look so great right now: he was actually sitting on the couch with red eyes staring blankly at the pause screen of Splatter-punk 3: The Rivening, but Alex didn't think that was informa-tion Aunt Dinah needed.

"All right. I'm glad to hear it. Thanks, Alex. I'll see you both soon."

"Yeah. Okay. Bye!" And Alex hung up.

Eddie was still staring at the screen. "You have to use the flaming sword on his toes. You'll never beat him with the battle-ax. And the toes are the only part with no armor."

"Um, okay."

"And please don't tell me anything my mom said, I know ex-actly what it was."

Alex didn't know what to say to that. He knew that Eddie was mad at his mom, but he usually sounded more sad than angry when he talked about her. Not tonight.

"So," Alex said, "toes. Flaming sword. Got it."

"Yeah, and if you need another tip, I've got Tanya's phone number in my bag."

"Aw, man, I'm not gonna call her! You know that, right?"

"I know. I know. I really can't blame you, or even her. I mean, I guess I'm not the kind of guy who . . . well, never mind."

Alex knew that this was the part where he was supposed to tell Eddie that he was really hot, that any girl would be lucky to have him, and maybe open up a pint of ice cream, but that was too girly, so all he said was "Naah, man, wrong girl, wrong time. That's all. Happens to me all the time."

"Yeah, but at least you get to kiss them before they dump you."

"Not always! Sometimes they actually laugh at me when I ask for their number. I figure it's their loss. Same deal here."

"I guess. I'm not mad at you, Alex, but I really don't feel like talking right now, you know?"

"Yeah."

"Can I finish this battle?"

"Yeah. Go ahead."

"Takin' your sloppy seconds," Eddie said, grinning, and Alex was shocked to hear Eddie say anything that raunchy. He watched as Eddie dispatched the level-four boss with three strokes of the flaming sword to the big toe and then watched in silent awe as Eddie spilled a spectacular amount of blood on his way to finishing levels five, six, and seven.

• • •

By breakfast, Eddie seemed pretty much like his normal self again. He showed off the sticker designs, and Alex told him they looked great. He really thought they were going to get an A on this project, which would be Alex's first A in high school. It felt good to realize that he had earned the grade, that nobody else on the team could have done what he'd done. Now they had a week to put it all together to look super-professional and impress the hell out of Lewis.

Or so they thought. Lewis, apparently, had other ideas. When they got to class, he didn't say anything for a long time, and everybody stared up at him, and it started to feel weird. Lewis kept looking like he was about to say something, but then he would stop. It was weird and disturbing to have some-body as tough and formal as Lewis looking like he was about to lose it. It made everything feel unpredictable—like, if this guy can act like this, who knows what else is going to happen?

Finally Lewis spoke. "Well. I have some bad news and some bad news. Do you want the bad news first? Good. Here it is. Due to a"—he paused here and took a breath and a pause that was a little too long—"family emergency, I will not be avail-able in school next Friday when your projects are due. Nor will I be here on Thursday." Long pause. "I will also be away from school for at least the next week, when your final marks for this quarter are due. And of course the following week is your spring vacation. What this means to you is as follows: your deadline has been pushed up to Wednesday."

Everybody in the class gasped at the same time, but nobody complained out loud because Lewis seemed so weird today and nobody wanted to be the one to set him off.

"I will say the following three things about this: One. Dead-lines do move in the business world. I once had a major cam-paign to present to a client who was called to Tokyo at the last minute and I had to work for twenty hours straight in order to take the campaign to the client on the airplane. I flew a to-tal of sixteen hours to Tokyo with an unpleasant bully of a man, slept for three hours on a couch in Narita airport, and flew home for another sixteen hours, arriving at Logan airport two hours before my original deadline. Two. What is happen-ing in my personal life at this moment is of such a serious na-ture that I will have no sympathy for complaints about a couple of late nights on your part and may indeed lose my pa-tience with anyone who is young, strong, and healthy com-plaining about losing a little sleep. Three. I am sorry."

Everybody in class just sat there for a minute letting every-thing Lewis said sink in. Alex couldn't decide what was more shocking: the fact that their project was due two days early, or the fact that Lewis had just apologized to the class.

Lewis broke the silence by saying, "You may use today's class time to touch base with your group."

After he left the room, somebody said, "Whoa." Savon was the first out of his seat, and he yelled out, "My group, over here." Alex was surprised that he didn't even want to make fun of him for being big Mr. Leader, because he felt like his chance at getting a good grade was slipping away. He was even more surprised to find that he actually did care. Weird.

Everyone pulled their chairs together over by Savon, and Alex looked around and saw the other groups in the class seemed worried. A couple of girls in different groups were crying.

"Okay, people, what's the plan?" Savon asked.

"Well, I gotta work, yo. I already did my part, so whatever we have now is gonna have to be good enough," Tanya said. Alex could see Eddie getting angry. After all, Eddie had done Tanya's part, and all he got in return was hurt and embarrassed. Alex saw an opportunity here to get one in for Eddie and, if he was lucky, make Tanya stop liking him.

"Yeah, who's gonna slap you so hard your whole family will feel it if you cost us an A? Oh, right, you didn't really do any work anyway. Never mind. Go braid some hair."

Somehow this came out meaner and less funny than he wanted it to. He must have been a little too excited about finally being on the giving end of one of those "You're lazy and we're sick of doing your work" comments. He wondered if being mean to Tanya would somehow hurt his chances with her cousin. After all, Tanya's hurting his cousin had ruined any chance she might have had with him, so maybe this would be it for Stephanie. Oh well.

While Alex pondered this, he watched Tanya turn beet red. Her fists were clenched tight. For a second, he thought she might hit him. Instead, she stood up, got up in Alex's face, and said, "You don't know *shit* about me or my life, so shut the hell up before you get smacked."

Then she turned around, grabbed her bag, and left.

"The love, people, the love," Savon said sadly as Tanya stormed out.

"Shoot, now we can get something done without her talking about I can't do this time, I can't do that time, my time is important. I'm tired of her." Everybody stared at Kenisha after she said this.

"Amen," Eddie said.

"Okay," Savon said, "so we're still gonna put her name on the project, mostly because I ain't got time to listen to her if we don't. So let's move ahead. The Web site is almost ready, and it really shouldn't be a problem to finish it over the weekend. I've just got to make sure we can get a report sent to somebody's phone straight from the site during our presentation. Speaking of which, even though he don't seem to have it workin' today, Alex is our smoothest talker."

"Hey, I got rid of her, didn't I? That was smooth!"

"No time to argue. You need to take the lead on the presentation. I was going to put you and Tanya on this, but why don't you handle it yourself?"

"Got it," Alex said, and he was surprised to find how much he was looking forward to this. He had sold the project to business owners he didn't know, and now he was going to get to do it in class. He'd do a good job and show Lewis that he wasn't a charming screw-up.

"That leaves the written part for Kenisha and Eddie," Savon said.

"The business plan is basically done," Kenisha said.

"And the promotional materials are done, but I don't have the explanation of the marketing strategy done yet," Eddie added, looking a little embarrassed.

"So you two get together and make sure we have a professional-looking written component."

"Okay," they both replied.

"All right. Our project is better than anybody else's, and we are going to get the highest grade in the short, sorry history of this school."

Alex smiled. He wanted to head over to Melville's with Eddie, but Eddie was already deep in conversation with Kenisha, so he decided to go by himself. He surprised himself by grabbing a notebook and a pen so he could make notes for his presentation.

As he walked out of the Parley Funds Tower, Alex felt really strange. It took him a minute to realize that he was going to Melville's to work, and not to scope out hot girls. With another minute's thought, he found he was actually glad the project had been moved up—it felt kind of good to be involved in something urgent and important. He'd never really felt this way before, but on this particular afternoon, he was excited and happy about school.

21

EDDIE MET KENISHA IN THE FA-CUE
Media Center right after school on Tuesday. The room was
filled with sophomores trying to finish their marketing projects. Eddie was glad Kenisha had gotten there early and saved
them a computer. She was typing away when Eddie entered,
and she turned, grabbed a couple of papers, and said, "Here,
would you mind triple-checking these? I spell-checked them
and proofread them and got my grandmom to look them over,
too, but it never hurts to have more eyes on something."

"Okay," Eddie said, and read over Kenisha's business plan. It
was easy to read but not dumbed down, and it was perfect except for a missing "is" on page 3.

"Wow!" Eddie said. "This looks fantastic. You're missing an
'is' here on page 3, though."

"Oh my God, thank you. I do not want any red ink on this."

Eddie lined up all his notes and began typing his marketing

strategy while Kenisha worked on graphs for the presentation. He felt a little self-conscious with Kenisha sitting right there while he typed, but she got out her graphing calculator and started doing stuff with the numbers Savon had given them on the cost of the Web hosting and bandwidth, the figures they'd gotten from the potential advertisers in Dudley Square and on Blue Hill Avenue, and their own estimates of what they would have to pay people to get them to reliably report "traffic problems" to the Web site every day.

Eddie typed an explanation of how the service would be marketed to its target audience and why they had chosen this kind of advertising. He wasn't used to doing his work in a public place like this, but there was something reassuring about it. All over the room, there was just the quiet clacking of keys as thirty kids sat at twenty-five computers busting their butts trying to get their projects done. It felt serious and important. Forty minutes later, Eddie had a few decent pages, which he printed and handed to Kenisha. He felt nervous and watched her face as she read what he'd written. She finished, read the pages again, paused, and then said, "I think this is very good, except for the second paragraph on the second page. It's not clear."

Eddie found himself getting defensive—of course it was clear! He wrote it! He got an A on everything! He had raised himself for over a year! He silently took the papers back and examined page 2 again and found Kenisha was right. Finally he finished, and then they looked over figures for the graphs.

"We need to put together a spreadsheet and some graphs to go with this. If we save the graphs on a disk, I can go to the copy shop before school tomorrow and print them in color, 'cause I don't trust this old printer not to start looking ghetto after everybody prints their projects," Kenisha said.

Eddie looked down at Kenisha's neat, clear notes and began setting up the spreadsheet. After about ten minutes, she said, "Um, Eddie, that looks great, would you mind saving it? It'll make me feel better." Okay, okay, he thought, and he wondered if he was this annoying when he was trying to get a good grade on a project. He saved it, and then he saved it again every five minutes, which was pretty much how often Kenisha reminded him to save it.

When he was done, he felt something wet smack the back of his neck. He removed the spitball, then looked around the computer room. Everybody seemed to be working. Then, just as he turned to face the computer, he saw Kelvin out of the corner of his eye spin around, put a straw to his lips, and shoot a spitball at Gisela's neck.

He then turned back around, along with everyone else in the room, as Gisela jumped up from her seat and said, "Damn! See, Kelvin, you play too much, that's why you're gonna get hurt!" Gisela looked angrier than Eddie had ever seen her, and she started walking over to Kelvin, who was laughing and saying, "Aaaaaah-haaaaaah! See, that's what you get! Ahhhhh-haaaaaah!" As Gisela advanced, Kelvin seemed to understand that she really was going to smack him, so he jumped up from his seat, said, "Time to bizzounce!" and promptly tripped over the front leg of his chair. As he put his hands out to break his fall, he pushed the switch on the power strip, and six computers turned off at once.

There were screams, and Kelvin was suddenly being threatened by several people instead of one, each promising to do really horrible things to Kelvin's face, family, and private parts.

The noise brought in Mr. Paulson, who Eddie guessed must actually live here, since nobody he knew had ever been here late enough to see him go home.

"What appears to be the difficulty?" Paulson yelled in his big, booming voice. There was silence for a second, and then everybody started talking at once, with variations on the phrase "behaving unprofessionally" popping out at least fifteen times.

Paulson reached down, switched the power strip back on, and turned to Kelvin. "Well, my young friend, it appears that your inability to conduct yourself in a professional manner may have adversely affected not only you but also your colleagues here. Let's go to my office and call your parents, shall we?" For once Kelvin didn't have a joke to crack, and he just hung his head as he left the room.

Once all the computers had rebooted, Eddie had to admit, if only to himself, that they had lost less work than anybody else because Kenisha had been bugging him about saving every five minutes.

As a result, they were able to get the spreadsheet done and the graphs generated in only another half hour, while several other people in the room were still retyping their documents. They packed up and headed out. Kenisha stuck her hand out and said, "Well, Eddie, I gotta say it's nice to work with somebody who actually does something for a change."

Eddie smiled. "I heard that."

"Well," Kenisha said, "I gotta go down to the office and try to use the phone to tell my grandmom I'm on my way. She won't let me get a cell, but she expects me to check in with her whenever I leave school late. It's a pain."

"I guess I should probably check in at home, too. I could probably get a phone, I just haven't bothered because"—because I don't know how long I'm staying, Eddie thought, but what he said was "I've been so busy, you know, new school and everything."

"Yeah," Kenisha said, and smiled. When they got to the office, Eddie strained to hear what was going on with Kelvin behind Paulson's closed door, but he couldn't make it out. Kenisha told him to use the phone on the secretary's desk first, so he picked it up and called home.

Alex answered. "Hello?"

"Hey, Alex, it's me," Eddie said.

"Why yes, I do happen to be the person who makes the decisions regarding phone service in this house!" Alex shouted.

"What?" Eddie said.

Alex kept shouting. "Please reveal to me all the advantages of your unlimited-calling plan!" Eddie could hear Uncle Brian in the background saying, "Don't torment the poor telemarketers!"

"Uh, Alex, what are you talking about?"

Alex whispered, "Your mom's here. I thought you should have some warning, and she's gonna want to talk to you if she knows you're on the phone. I'm gonna tell them you sent me a text message from school, and you're tied up, but you'll be home soon. Take as much time as you need, but call my cell next time. She's, uh, she's spending the night, so you can't really wait her out."

Eddie stared into space.

"Eddie?"

"Okay, thanks, Alex," Eddie said blankly.

"Ah, but what about my in-state toll calls?" Alex bellowed. "For I have a different lady friend at every exit off the Turnpike, from Stockbridge to Boston, as the James Taylor song my mother is so fond of . . . Hello? Hello?" and he hung up.

Eddie put the phone down, sat on the floor in front of the desk, and put his head in his hands.

"You okay?" Kenisha said.

Eddie had no idea how to answer that question. Was he okay? Well, he was going to get a really good grade on the biggest project of the year. He was, up until two minutes ago, happier than he had been in a long time. And now Mom was back, and she was going to want him to leave, and how was he going to tell her that he didn't want to? And would Aunt Lily and Uncle Brian even let him stay? Would they want him? They told him they loved him all the time, and they did seem to like him, and it couldn't hurt that he was way less trouble than Alex. But did that mean they'd be willing to fight for him? Probably not.

He must have been quiet for a long time because Kenisha bent down next to him and asked, "Eddie? Did you hear me?"

"Yeah, I'm sorry, I . . . uh . . ." And before he could finish thinking please don't cry in front of a girl, he found himself choking up and saying, "My mom's out of rehab, okay, and I don't want to see her and I don't want to go back with her and I hate her and I hate that." He sunk his head back into his hands. "Sorry. I didn't mean to say that, and I know nobody wants to hear about it."

"It's okay. Hey, listen, are you hungry?"

"Uh . . . I think I was a minute ago."

" 'Cause when I feel bad, I mean, I usually feel worse if I'm hungry, of course I have to have a snack every two hours or I get mad cranky anyway, high metabolism or something, but anyway, maybe you should eat something before you go home."

Eddie picked up his head. "Yeah. Yeah, that sounds good. I have to figure out what to say to her, or at least get myself ready to see her."

"Okay, let me call my grandmom here, and we'll go find something to eat." Eddie listened as Kenisha talked to her grandmother. "Hi, Grandmom. No, I'm still working . . . Yes, I had my part done yesterday . . . No, I know, Grandmom, but I can't pick who I'm in a group with . . ." She looked apologetically at Eddie as she said this. "Yes, Grandmom. No more than an hour. I know. Yes. Well, I have to come all the way down to the office to call you. Now, if I had a cell phone . . . No ma'am. Yes ma'am. Yes ma'am. Okay." Kenisha rolled her eyes and hung up the phone. "I love her, but she is mad strict. She needs to chill. She's afraid I'm gonna end up like my mom, I guess."

Eddie wasn't sure if he should ask, but he figured he'd already told Kenisha his secret, so he said as he was getting up, "How's that?"

"I don't know," Kenisha said as they walked toward the elevator. "She had me when she was sixteen, and she's in Los Angeles now trying to be some kind of actress, but mostly she waits tables, which she could do here if she cared about me at all."

Eddie didn't know what to say about that, so he didn't say anything. They headed out of school in search of food, but it was already close to seven, and Boston's financial district was practically a ghost town after six. Finally Kenisha said there was always something open at South Station, so they went there and got slices of bad pizza and sat in hard plastic chairs.

As soon as he started eating, Eddie realized he was starving. He ate his two slices in about a minute and got two more. They both attacked their food and didn't really speak. Eddie enjoyed thinking only about pizza for a few minutes.

But then, of course, he had to stop eating eventually. When he was done, Kenisha looked at him. "I guess you were hungry."

Eddie blushed. "Yeah, I guess so. I always feel better after I eat. But I still don't feel good."

"I hear you. Sometimes I don't feel too good about going home either. It's mad boring at my house, and my grandmom is so strict . . . Oh, I'm sorry," Kenisha said. "I should shut up about my problems, I know you got problems of your own."

"That's okay. I kinda like hearing about somebody else's problems. Sometimes I feel like I'm the only person in the world with messed-up stuff going on at home." Neither one of them spoke for a minute. "Well, I guess I should go see my mom. Or maybe I'll go see if I can get beat up on the street or something so I can go to the hospital instead."

Kenisha smiled. "Yeah, that financial district crew is hard-core, yo. Don't be wearin' the wrong bank's colors down here."

Eddie laughed. "Ugh. What am I gonna say to her?"

"I don't know. My mom calls every week, and I never know what to say to her. Sometimes I think she just calls so she can feel like she's not a terrible mom, and it doesn't have anything to do with me."

"Yeah. I feel the same way. I mean, what my mom's gonna say is that she wants me back, and it's not because it's better for me to live with her, it's just that she feels better about herself that way. Like she didn't really screw up her life that bad if her son is there."

They were quiet for a minute. "Well," Kenisha finally said, "I better get my butt home."

"Yeah, I guess I have to see her sometime."

"Listen," Kenisha said, reaching into her book bag and ripping a piece of paper out of a notebook, "if you want to talk about it, give me a call. I just convinced her to let me talk to boys on the phone." She handed Eddie her number. "Not that it's happened"—Kenisha laughed nervously—"but you know, I had to stand up for the principle."

"I hear you. Thanks," Eddie said. "See you tomorrow."

Even though he was dreading going home, he felt a little bit lighter for having unloaded his big secret on somebody besides Alex.

Maybe he would call her when this was over. It was nice

talking to somebody who kind of understood his life. Alex was great, but he had two pretty stable parents and just couldn't really understand the way somebody like Kenisha could.

Eddie suddenly realized something with a shock. He might call Kenisha because Kenisha, who was a girl, and pretty, and nice, had given him her phone number. In spite of everything, he found himself smiling.

He took the piece of paper out of his pocket and waved it around to the empty street, and called out, laughing, "Digits, baby!"

22

ALEX WAS ON THE COUCH PLAYING
Splatterpunk 3: The Rivening. He was doing horribly, partly because he was also trying to overhear his mom's conversation with Aunt Dinah in the kitchen. His stomach felt so tight and acidy that he felt like he might actually puke.

He could only imagine how Eddie felt. He really didn't want to be there, but he had to have Eddie's back tonight. Even if Eddie didn't want Alex in the room when he talked to his mom, he might want to talk to Alex later. Or maybe Eddie would want him in the room if Mom and Aunt Dinah were tag-teaming him about how he had to go back to Oldham. It might help Eddie to have a smooth talker on his side.

Alex was so distracted he didn't really pay attention to his game and caused poor Mace Hardcastle to have his flesh ripped from his bones by the level-five army of the undead yet again.

Finally he heard the elevator and dropped the controller and stood up. Aunt Dinah, Mom, and Dad all came running, then stood there trying to pretend like they just happened to be standing right by the elevator. Under different circumstances, Alex would've thought it was funny.

The doors slid open as Eddie hauled on the strap on the inside, and he stepped into the loft looking kind of lost and scared. Alex wanted to jump up, push Eddie back into the elevator, and run away. Instead, he just stood there looking stupid like his mom and dad.

Aunt Dinah was crying, and she went over to Eddie, hugging him and bawling. Alex watched as Eddie received the hug stiffly, just like he did when Mom hugged him.

And then he noticed that Eddie was shaking, his face was scrunched up, and that tears were pouring down his cheeks. Alex felt embarrassed, like maybe this was too private for him to see. But he couldn't just go to his room, and anyway the walls were so thin that you could hear everything.

Finally Aunt Dinah pulled away, and Eddie stood there still looking all stiff and red-faced. Alex was surprised to find that he wanted to hug him himself.

Of course, he didn't. Everybody stared at poor Eddie until Aunt Dinah put her arm around his shoulder, and said, "So, um, listen. We need to talk." Then she started crying again, and they both just stood there hugging and crying for what felt like an hour to Alex. He glanced over at his mom and dad, and they just gave him these "I don't know what to do either" looks.

Eventually Eddie and Aunt Dinah made their way over to

the couch. Alex had forgotten to pause his game, and Mace Hardcastle was screaming, "My flesh! My very soul!" as he got killed again.

"Uh, let me just get that," Alex said, and stumbled over to the TV and turned off the PS2. There was loud static and snow all over the TV screen, and Alex snapped that off, too.

"So, Eddie, you got my letter," Aunt Dinah said.

"Yeah," Eddie said. It was the first sound he'd made since he came home.

"So you know how sorry I am, how sorry I will always be for everything that happened—no, for everything I did. It didn't just happen. They had to keep reminding me about that, you know, I sort of, I thought of this whole thing like a terrible thunderstorm, something that just happened to us, but of course it wasn't a thunderstorm, it was something I did."

Eddie didn't say anything. Mom was motioning for Alex and Dad to go to the kitchen, but Alex didn't want to leave Eddie alone, so he looked at his mom quizzically, pretending he didn't understand what her hand motions meant.

"It's okay, Lily," Aunt Dinah said, "you've been more of a parent to Eddie in the last couple months than I was for years, so we're all in this together at this point."

"All right," Mom said, but she sure didn't look like it was all right.

"So listen, Eddie," Aunt Dinah said, while stroking Eddie's hair like he was a little kid. Eddie looked like he wanted to push her hand away, but he just sat there taking it. "I screwed up, and I know I screwed up, and that's what makes this so hard for me. I know . . . I know that you . . ." She sat there for a moment trying to compose herself. Alex thought about how scenes like this were always way better on TV sitcoms, where people screamed for two minutes and then hugged for ten seconds while the studio audience went "Awwwww," and then they made a joke and everything was fine just in time for the last tampon commercial.

Aunt Dinah went on. "I know that you . . . that you want us to be together, *deserve* to have a normal life with a normal mom and everything. And that's why . . ." She took a deep breath and paused before continuing. "That's why, even though I know you want that and you deserve that, and I'm done with drugs, I'm not—I'm working really hard to stay sober, one day at a time, just like they say, but I just . . . Well, I don't have enough money to get a new place in Oldham, and, anyway, I don't think it's going to be good for my sobriety to be on the North Shore, I mean, there are all those places, all the people.

"So I just feel awful about this, Eddie, about uprooting you again, about not being able to get you back to your real home, but, well, Lily and Brian have generously offered to let me stay here until I get on my feet, you know, get enough money together for first and last months' rent so we can get an apartment."

Aunt Dinah kind of choked up again. "I mean, it won't be as nice a place as this, or as the old house, but we'll get something of our own soon, I promise. But that means, for the meantime, we'll have to stay in Boston, sweetie, and I'm sorry about that, I know you must really want to go back to Oldham, but I'm afraid that part of our lives is really over now.

I'm sorry, sweetie, I'm so sorry." Aunt Dinah looked like it just about killed her to say this, and Alex actually kind of wanted to give her a hug and tell her it was okay.

Instead, Eddie did it. "It's okay, Mom," he said. His voice sounded weird and strangled, but it wasn't the same strangled voice he used when he was trying not to cry. Eddie reached over and gave Aunt Dinah a hug that lasted a long time and was embarrassing, at least to Alex.

Then Eddie stood up, and said, still in that weird strangled voice, "Alex, you wanna take a walk with me?"

"Sure, of course," Alex said and jumped up. They went over to the elevator. Alex swung the heavy doors closed and looked over at Eddie, who wouldn't say anything or look at him. When Alex swung the doors open at the ground floor, Eddie looked over at him and started laughing. Really, really loud. "I was so . . . oh my God, I've been so worried for so long—" and he had to stop because he was laughing so hard, "I was so afraid, I thought she was gonna . . ." More laughter. " 'I'm so sorry you don't get to go back to Oldham' "—he almost choked he was laughing so hard—"I was like yeah Mom I was gonna . . . scream at you if you tried to make me . . ." and he just collapsed on the floor of the elevator laughing.

And now that it was finally over, the tension of the whole night, the tension of Eddie's whole stay here, was over, at least for now, Alex found that Eddie's laughter was pretty contagious, and he started laughing, too. The whole thing was just so damn sad it was funny, or maybe it was just so funny it was funny. Eddie had been getting all geared up to yell at his mom about something and she had been getting all geared up to let

Eddie down easy, and when you thought about it even for a second it made you laugh, but especially with Eddie laughing so hard that tears were coming out of his eyes. It was hilarious in a weird way, and then the elevator door started trying to close on Eddie's foot, and it kept popping back open, and the elevator started buzzing, and that was funny, too.

23

EVERYBODY SPOKE IN THE PRESEN-
tation, but nobody spoke as much as Alex, and Eddie was in
awe of him. He was definitely Mr. Smooth: he made jokes that
even Lewis laughed at, he answered every question clearly and
confidently, and five kids asked him how they could sign up
for the traffic report at the end of the class.

Lewis applauded, and the entire group got to come to the
front of the class as he said, "At the outset of this assignment,
several of you approached me and asked exactly what my
grading standard would be, what, in effect, an A would look
like. I told you that as no one had ever received an A on this
project, I believed it was actually impossible to do so. Now, I
will need to give the written materials a thorough appraisal,
and I daren't even speculate on what kind of grade I will give
those, but I'm happy to report that today, I have seen my first

A-quality presentation on this project. Fantastic work, all of you."

For the first time since Dad died, Eddie actually felt like stuff was starting to go his way. Even when Mom got enough money for an apartment, they'd never have to go back to Old-ham, so he could stay here, where he had friends and a family and all the stuff he'd thought he'd have to wait till college or even later to get.

After class, Savon yelled out, "Yo, my group over here!" and everybody, including Tanya, smiled and went over to him, even though technically there was no more group because the project was over.

"I just want to thank everybody for coming through on this," Savon said. "Y'all did a fantastic job, and I think we should think about setting this thing up for real after fourth quarter. The hard part is already done, and all we'd need is a server and a broadband connection, and some traffic re-porters. Obviously we ain't doing this right now, but think about it for the summer. I think we could make some bills."

Eddie thought about how cool it would be if this became a real thing. And how cool it would be to have a job and some money he could use to, say, take Kenisha out or something.

"Anyway," Savon went on, "thank you. I'm proud of us."

"Yo, I got something to say," Tanya said. Everybody looked at her, and Eddie was afraid she was going to rip into Alex for being nasty to her. Instead she said, "I'm sorry to everybody but especially Left Eye, for not pulling my weight. I had mad stuff going on in the last few days, and though everything is okay now, I'm sorry y'all had to carry me. But thank you for doing it." Were her eyes actually tearing up there? Well, Eddie knew about having "mad stuff" going on in your life, and he instantly forgave her for not pulling her weight. He thought it would probably take a while longer to forgive her for liking Alex, even though he found he didn't like her like that anymore anyway.

Everybody kind of mumbled that it was fine, and Alex said, "Uh, listen, Tanya, I was mad stressed the other day, and you know, I'm sorry I was mean."

"That's okay," Tanya said softly, and she even smiled.

"That's what I'm talking about, people, the love! The love!" Savon said, and everybody kept grinning these big goofy grins and started packing up their stuff.

Eddie noticed that Kenisha seemed to be packing up extra-slow, so he dropped his notebook and found that he had a bunch of papers in his folder that he had to organize before he could leave. Eventually he and Kenisha were the only ones left in the classroom. He could hear Alex in the hallway going, "Yo, Harry, guess which advisory group got the best marketing presentation grade in the whole history of FA-CUE?"

Harrison must have been happy, because he didn't say anything to Alex about calling him Harry or about using the school's full acronym, and Eddie could hear him fading down the hall going, "Excellent! Hey, that is fantastic! I'm really proud of you."

Kenisha looked at Eddie and smiled. "So," she said, "how'd it go with your mom?"

"It went okay. I mean, it was hard to see her. It was actually really hard to see her. She told me she was sorry but we could probably never go back to Oldham and we'd both have to stay in Boston at least till the end of the school year and maybe even longer."

"Hey, that's great!" Kenisha said, then stopped and said, "I mean, it is, isn't it?"

"It totally is. I feel way more at home here than I ever did in Oldham, and I think it's gonna be . . . I don't know, it's just gonna be easier for me to forgive her if we don't have to go back to the same place where everything sucked so bad, where she was . . . you know, where she wanted drugs more than anything."

"Yeah. Even if my mom wanted me to move to California, there is no way I could do it right now. But I still wish she'd ask."

"Yeah," Eddie said. He didn't have anything else to say, so he didn't say anything at all, and that was all right. That was a great thing about hanging out with Kenisha. She was kind. And smart. And, Eddie thought, pretty. He liked the fact that her glasses made her look as smart as she actually was.

They walked into the hall, and Eddie was feeling better and more confident than he had felt in his whole life: they'd just aced their project, and he was surprised to find he was looking forward to seeing Mom tonight. Maybe they could start to have some kind of normal relationship, and even if they couldn't, she never shut up about how proud of him she was, and that was definitely nice.

He thought about asking Kenisha if she wanted to go out and get some coffee or something (because, having consumed one free latte in his whole life, he was now a cool coffee-drinkin' man), but he suddenly got afraid, and he didn't want to ruin the best day he'd had in years by getting rejected. So he just said, "Well, uh, see you tomorrow, I guess."

Kenisha smiled. "Yeah, you will. I keep telling Grandmom I should get a day to play hooky, but she's not buying it."

Eddie laughed, because he knew Kenisha playing hooky was about as likely as him playing hooky. And then he risked rejection even though he thought he'd already decided not to do that. "So, uh . . . can I like . . . call you tonight or something?"

"Yeah," Kenisha said, smiling, and then Eddie couldn't say anything else because he was thinking about how beautiful she looked when she smiled.

After school, Eddie went to therapy and told Don everything that was going on, and for the first time ever, he didn't feel heavy and sad at the end of their session. He still went to his room when he got back home, but only because he knew that everybody would give him a few minutes alone after therapy, and that would give him a great opportunity to call Kenisha. He smiled at his deviousness, even as he thought that he really needed his own phone. But he'd feel bad asking Aunt Lily and Uncle Brian, and Mom was currently destitute. Well, maybe he'd apply for a job at Melville's or something. That way he could earn money for dates.

Kenisha could only talk for ten minutes before her grandmom started telling her to get off, but it felt good to talk to her, even though it felt a lot more awkward than any of their conversations ever had before.

When Eddie and Alex got to advisory the next morning, the

door was open, and they could hear Harrison's voice. They looked at each other. It was still fifteen minutes before school started. This couldn't be good.

Except it was. Harrison was sitting there with a big grin on his face in front of bags of bagels, doughnuts, and munchkins, and a couple of boxes of coffee, and everybody was walking around eating and smiling.

"What's going on?" Eddie asked, and Kelvin said, "Yo, Harry—"

Mr. Harrison cut him off with "This is a professional celebration, Kelvin, so let's have some professional language, please."

Kelvin rolled his eyes, and said, "Mr. Harrison is rewarding us because our advisory got the best grades on the marketing presentation."

"That's right!" Mr. Harrison said loudly as he moved right next to the open door. He yelled down the hall, "Yes, though certain of my colleagues have expressed concern about how this advisory is conducted, it appears that this advisory outperformed all others on the biggest academic task of the year!" He turned back to the room, smiling.

"So what did you guys get?" Alex asked Gisela.

"B plus. Second highest grade in the class," Gisela said, smiling. "No thanks to a certain person who caused a last-minute power failure."

"And then stayed up all night fixing everything," Kelvin called out.

"All right, all right, I guess I have to give you that," Gisela said.

"And I did practically the whole presentation," Hanh called out.

"Good job," Alex said, and for a minute, Eddie thought he was going to add something snotty about how she didn't have any distractions, but, shockingly, he just left it at that. Hanh and Kenisha huddled in the corner and whisperered. Were they looking at him?

The rest of the day felt like an afterthought, even though Harrison bought them pizza for lunch. When school ended, Alex asked if he wanted to head straight home. Eddie said, "No thanks. I think I'm gonna hang out and try to get some homework done here, so I don't have my mom looking over my shoulder asking me a million questions now that she's involved in my life again."

Alex laughed. "Okay, then," he said, and headed out.

Eddie wandered the hall aimlessly for a minute, hoping to catch sight of Kenisha. Finally, when he made his third trip past the advisory door, he saw her standing in the hall. He reached down inside himself and clamped his fear in a tight little ball, and then stood off to the side and watched as this kind of happy, very confident, not-too-bad-looking kid replaced the sad, shy, hideous kid that had lived in his skin for so long. Then he watched as the happy kid who was actually him said to Kenisha, "So, um, do you wanna go get some coffee or something?"

"Oh, I can't," Kenisha said, and Eddie's stomach fell. All of a sudden the shy kid was back, and he was yelling at Eddie see, he knew he was a loser, why did he even try? "I'm . . . I had a little argument with my grandmom last night, and I guess I

was disrespectful or something, 'cause now I'm on punish-
ment for a week."

"Oh, jeez, I'm sorry," Eddie said.

"Thanks. I think it was worth it. It felt good to tell her she
should trust me a little more. Still, it's too bad—I mean . . ."
she trailed off as they reached the elevator, then said, "I don't
feel like waiting for that thing all day. I'm gonna take the
stairs."

Eddie didn't think it ever took all day for the elevator to
come, but he decided to follow Kenisha anyway. "Uh, sure, I
could use some exercise," he said as he followed her into the
stairwell.

When he got through the fire door to the stairwell, he saw
Kenisha waiting. She had taken her glasses off. Eddie stopped
short, and Kenisha leaned down and gave him a really nice, really slow, kiss with her soft, soft lips, and before Eddie could
figure out what was happening, she bolted down the stairs.
"Call me!" she called out.

"I will!" Eddie responded. He took a moment to collect
himself. When he got out onto the street, he saw Alex and
Tanya standing on the sidewalk talking. Tanya handed Alex a
piece of paper and walked away, and Alex stood there smiling.

"Alex!" Eddie called out.

Alex looked at him and immediately got this guilty look on
his face. "Oh, hey, Eddie, I thought you were studying. I
mean, I was just, you know, I felt like I had to apologize again,
because I actually felt bad about being mean to her, and before I knew what was happening, she's giving me her number.
I mean, you're my boy, well, no, you're family, and that's more

important, and there is no way I'm calling her. You know I wouldn't do you like that, right?"

Eddie was touched, and also kind of amused. Tanya was just about the furthest thing from his mind right now. "Don't worry about it," Eddie said. "It's cool with me, although you're probably going to have to pick between her and Stephanie."

"I don't know. I was thinking we could get like a vat of Jell-O or something and they could fight it out over me."

Eddie laughed. "Don't cheat on Tanya. I'm way too busy to visit you in the hospital."

Alex smiled. "Yeah, you might be right about that. I guess I'll have to pick one. Now that is a problem. Oh, jeez, I'm sorry, man, I'm talking about picking between Tanya and Stephanie. I mean, I'm really only joking about that, Tanya's hot and all, but she kind of terrifies me. And it might be just easier to date somebody you didn't have to see in school all the time. Seems like that would give me less opportunity to piss her off, which I guess I do to girls without even trying. Maybe that happens to everybody. But in any case, it's still a good idea. You know, the more I think of it, the more I think about it, the more I think it's got to be Stephanie. It's a shame that the Jello-O wrestling isn't gonna happen, though. But anyway, it'll do Tanya some good to get rejected, especially after you—"

"Just came from the stairwell, if you know what I mean," Eddie said, and smiled.

Alex's mouth fell open. "You? Wait a minute. What? Who?

Wait," and Eddie smiled and started walking toward the bus stop. "No, wait!" Alex said.

The bus pulled up, and Eddie got on, with Alex right behind him, still going, "You have to tell me! We're family!"

The doors closed behind them, the bus pulled away, and Eddie and Alex were on their way home.